Water Wishes

ELIZABETH YORK

Dear Daddy,

It has nearly been six years since you have been gone and I am still working to make you proud. I got to see my son for the first time in five years. He is so much like you, daddy. He is brave, strong, and forgives in spades to everyone who has wronged him.

I promise to get him back. My kids are my everything, and you did the best you could for as long as you had on this earth with him, and now it is my turn to be his parent. I will never stop fighting for him as you never stopped fighting for me.

There isn't a day that goes by that I don't miss you and need you in my world, but in your absence I will continue to work to make you proud.

Support Cancer Awareness

Dedications

Laura – You have been a friend since the beginning. You give love as you get it and that makes you an amazing person. I will never be able to thank you for bringing me in and having faith in me.

Kimmy – *Agent K* – I love the hell out of you. When I am having the worst day ever I know I can come to you or silently scroll-stalk you and I will be laughing till I am in tears. You take the time and give me feedback to make me be better and strive to get it right the first time.

Kris – You and I have been friends from the beginning. You were the first blogger I ever talked to and you popped my review cherry, but then I got to know you and we became so much more. I love you for that.

Ena & Amanda – You have to share a dedication. I know I know so unfair, but here is why... Because I want to say the same thing to both of you. You both ROCK! I have never been so happy to work with you two.

For my Fans - I love that you get me. I love that you stalk me in a healthy-non-violent way. You keep me grounded and for that I thank you all.

Finally, for my Family – To my kids: you are dedicated in every book because you are my life. I love you whole- heartedly. To my husband: who makes me laugh and takes my chair away to get me to stop working so hard. I couldn't write a better man than you. For my mom, and step-dad: Thank you for believing I could do this. For everyone related by blood or friendship. I love you all. Your support is everything to me, and am so glad you are in my life.

Prologue

"Who presents this woman to be married to this man?" the chaplain asked.

"On behalf of all who have gathered here, and all of those not able to be with us today, I do." My dad spoke with a gravelly voice from his unshed tears. Then he gave me a kiss and put my hand in Jax's. "Take care of her, Jax."

"I won't ever let her go," he replied, then winked at me.

The chaplain said another prayer in which Jax and I never looked away from each other. Then the wedding moved forward. My mind faded down memory lane as the chaplain talked about rings and marriage. Brooklyn tapped me and took my bouquet when she handed me Jax's ring.

"Jax, I promise to love you all day, every day, for the rest of our days. I promise to make you angry and be a sore loser. I even promise to mess up the house, but I promise I will be worth the headache. I promise that there will be more good times than bad, and I will always make sure when something is bad that I give you something good to go with it. I promise to always make water wishes with you. You made me whole again, and I promise to stand by you every day for as long as we both shall live."

Then I slid the ring onto his finger. The laughter that had filled the air from my vows was almost a sigh of relief as I turned into a basket case.

"Candice, I promise to love you more than I have ever loved anyone. I promise to put you above all others. I promise to let you have the last bite of my banana split waffles. I promise that I will get you coffee every morning, and tuck you in beside me every night. I promise not to get mad when you make a mess, and I promise to make you as angry as you make me, because I can promise that I will always apologize, and I promise we will make up. I can't promise you the world, but I can promise you that I will spend my life trying to make you happy. I promise never to purposely make you cry. I love you and will love you as long as we both shall live."

Jax slid my ring on as the tears started to fall. The chaplain went on talking about how two people were becoming one, as I stared into Jax's gray eyes tinged with light blue strands. He was my wish, my water wish. He was everything I wasn't and that made us whole.

"You may now kiss the bride," the chaplain said loudly, and Jax pulled me in for a kiss. When his lips first pressed down on mine, there was an odd clapping sound that made me pull away.

"Did I miss the party?"

Shivers traveled down my spine as I stared into Jax's eyes. He turned his head and then looked back at me in disbelief. I swallowed hard and closed my eyes. I knew that voice, but it wasn't possible.

Chase stood at the back of the church, while people murmured and gasped. He looked like he hadn't changed a bit. Shock reverberated through me and I wondered if this was a dream. I pulled my hand out of Jax's and pinched my arm, but I didn't wake up.

"Come on, Jax, the bet is over," Chase bellowed over the gasping crowd.

"Bet? What bet?"

Water Wishes

I sat in my favorite swing at the park that held Chase's name on the sign and wondered how I got here. How did I wind up married to my fiancé's best friend? How did I find myself with a husband who, even though he used me in a bet, I couldn't find myself angry with him?

I watched the sun setting in the distance while children ran around me in my wedding dress. I left my husband at the alter when I could no longer find a single breath. I left Chase to stand there and defend himself and explain his actions to everyone but me, when I really wanted to know where he had been.

When I fled like a sheep who had spotted a wolf in the woods, I didn't bother to look back. I didn't mention to Jax where I was going. I didn't stay and tell Chase I didn't want him anymore. I didn't tell him I was happy. I had gotten really good at running when things got hard, and while I thought I had gotten better, today had proved I hadn't grown much at all.

"Excuse me." A little girl wearing a pink jumper with blond pig tails stopped next to the swing set. I brought my swing to a full halt and looked over and gave her a smile. "Are you a princess?" she asked, and I chuckled.

"No sweetie, I'm not a princess," I replied, and she fiddled with her hands as I used to do as a child when I was nervous.

"Then why are you wearing your dress in the park?" She asked and I stood up out of the red swing and walked over and bent down in front of her.

"I am a bride. This is my wedding dress," I explained, but it only led to more questions.

"Where is your husband?" She asked softly as she turned and picked up a tiny yellow flower off the ground, placing it in my hair.

"I don't know where he is right now," I smiled as she grabbed my hand and looked at my wedding rings.

"Did your husband run away?" She asked and I tilted my head as a sadness invaded her eyes. "My dad ran away from my mom and me."

"What is your name?" I asked as she played with my rings.

"I'm Dani," she explained.

"Hi Dani. I am Candice, but you can call me Candy," I whispered and she looked up and gave me a smile. "Are you sad that your dad ran away?" I asked, and Dani nodded her head as her blue eyes filled with tears.

"My husband didn't run from me. I ran from him," I explained and she halted her tears as confusion took over her facial expressions.

"Why would you run away? Did you not love him?" She asked and I had to wonder if she was really asking why I left or if she was looking for a reason her own dad left.

"I love him very much, but I was afraid," I spoke softly. "When people get scared, sometimes they run to what they feel is safe."

"You feel safe at the park?" Dani asked, and I looked over at the grey stone wishing well Jax had built me and the park bench that sat near it. I could still see him saying he wanted to marry me as he stood beside it. I took in my lighthouse, as it called people home with its light, and the waves crashed into the wall around it as the inlet flooded water into the ocean.

"This is my favorite place to be when I am sad or afraid. I played at this park when I was your age and it makes me happy. When you are sad, what do you do?" I asked, but she shrugged her shoulders. Then she picked up another flower and placed it in my hand.

"Dani, did you know that my swing is magic. It makes fears disappear. Do you think if I share my favorite swing with you, it might help you feel better?"

She smiled at me as she nodded and then skipped around me into the swing I had climbed out of. I pushed her in the swing until she began swinging higher on her own. When I looked toward the parking lot, I saw my husband leaning up against his white F-250, still wearing his tux with the tie untied.

I took a few steps across the sand, picking up my silver high heels I had worn in the wedding, and took a deep breath. I knew he would want an explanation and I had none. I started to walk off when Dani called my name. She quickly slowed the swing and nearly jumped out. Then she ran to me and wrapped her arms around my hips and give me a hug.

"Don't be afraid of him, Candy. He looks ready to marry you," Dani spoke up as she looked over and saw Jax. "He is your prince, and you are his princess."

"Do you think he would stay married to me, even though I ran?" I asked, and she chewed over the question as if she were an adult herself.

"My mom says everyone deserves to have their story heard and be granted forgiveness. I think he wants to marry you. Why else would he be in your safe place?"

Dani's mom called her name and told her it was time to go home. As she started to run off, she turned back and took the flower she had placed in my hand and ran over and gave it to Jax. I watched him say something and then she gave me a thumbs up and I laughed.

If only life were as simple as being seven years old again. I slowly walked across the park until I was standing about fifteen feet from Jax. I couldn't look him in the eye. I didn't even know what to say.

"I thought you might be out here," Jax stated, as if explaining that he had been looking for me. I merely nodded my head and stared at the ground. "I know it was a shock to see Chase again. To be honest, I thought I was dreaming."

Tears welled up in my eyes as I thought back to that moment in the church. The split second when everything got really hard really fast. Chase had walked in and when I finally rasped out a question and asked him why he was there and how his reply gutted, left me broken, and running for the park.

"I got shot, and when I met with God, I begged him for just a little more time with you. When I woke up, I healed. I finished the job I was on, and I came back for you. I was allowed to come back for you because fate said I loved you enough. What we shared was not supposed to end so early. We have been given a second chance at happiness."

Even thinking about what he said left me with more questions than answers, but I wasn't sure I wanted to know.

"It sounds bad, but I hoped I was dreaming, or thought maybe I had a brain tumor. Anything would have been better than what happened," I whispered, trying to hide my quivering lip.

"Do you love him?" Jax asked as I silently hoped and prayed he wouldn't ask me that.

"I don't know."

"Do you love me?" Jax cleared his throat and I finally met his grey eyes to see they were clouded behind redness. His heart was on his sleeve and he thought I was about to end the love story that made us who we were.

"Yes, I do love you," I replied, hoping that would be enough, but his face said it wasn't.

"Then why are you standing so far away? You could drive a car between us."

I took a small step forward and a tear fell from my eye. I knew when I ran out of the church that I had hurt a lot of people, including Jax, but I didn't know what else to do.

"Why did you run?" Jax asked, and I took a deep breath, hoping like hell I could convey what was happening in my head when I headed for the side door of the church and stole the limo.

"One minute, I'm in the church marrying you and making my heart whole. The next minute, I am in the park because my heart stopped beating and I couldn't breathe," I wiped a tear that fell and hoped he could translate what I was trying to say.

"It shocked the hell out of me too, but you just bailed. You didn't wait for an explanation. You just ran away from everyone who loves you. Where are you now? Are you still running?"

I took a few steps forward and placed my rings in his hand. Thunder sounded in the background as I swallowed hard.

"I don't know where I am."

Chapter 2

I found myself at Brooklyn's apartment drenched to the bone and needing clothes. Thankfully, we were near the same size. I changed into a pair of her jeans and a red tank top.

I peeked out the door of the bedroom to see Mark with his brown hair and blue eyes towering over Brooklyn with his wide shouldered muscular build. I towel dried my hair as the iPod took me back in time to when I was a child watching the Disney Movie *Aladdin*.

The singer echoed about new worlds and diamond skies as Mark held out his hand and Brooklyn took it. He spun her out and her black hair flowed in the wind as he pulled her back into his arms and they began dancing.

I watched in awe as they each sang their parts and laughed, their love filling the room. They made it look so easy, and left me envious of what they got to share. They were what real love should look like. Neither of them ran, or were terrified of losing the other. They seemed like they had been designed from a catalogue to fit together.

As a new song began, a knock sounded on Brooklyn's door. I stopped leering and walked over to her navy blue couch. Then both Brooklyn and Mark's phones went off. Mark immediately checked his phone. Then he and Brooklyn shared an ominous look. I felt nauseous. The door knockers are never who you want them to be.

"Candice," Brooklyn started as she walked over to me with her phone. "I know you need a break, but this is standing outside my door." She showed me her phone where the security outside her door had photographed him.

"Shit," I spoke out loud and then covered my mouth. "Let him in, I guess."

Brooklyn went to the door and allowed Chase to enter, but then she did her own WWE Diva move and him pinned up against the light colored wall in her entryway before it opened up into the room.

"You make her shed one single tear and I will kill you. Then I will have you stuffed, bronzed, and put in my dad's garden for target practice!"

Chase nodded his understanding as Brooklyn let him go. Mark turned off the iPod by remote and stood stoic as Chase walked across the hardwood into the living area.

"How did you find me?" I asked as Brooklyn stepped away from him.

"I heard you and Brooklyn were friends. I thought if I came here and you weren't here then she would know where you were. Can we talk?" Chase asked, but Mark decided to answer for me.

"You can talk from there. Voices carry in this apartment so she can hear you just fine from right there."

"Candice, that is not how I intended to come back. I mean, I did, but-," Chase started, and I took in his Mets t-shirt and jeans. He looked comfortable, even if he was wearing the wrong team, but his stuttering said this was hard for him. "I wanted to approach you quietly and talk, but-,"

"Where have you been?" I asked softly, interrupting his speech I saw coming from a mile away.

"Deep undercover," Chase replied, but I was having trouble believing him and he must have seen it because he lifted his shirt to show me that across his rippled stomach were multiple scars.

"You really got shot," I pointed out my observation as I watched him lower his shirt.

"I want to be with you, if you will have me. I was serious in the church. You brought me back from the dead."

Brooklyn walked over with a 'yeah right' look on her face, joining Mark as he stood between us.

"You had a baby with Christina," I spoke up, cutting him off from whatever he was about to say next.

"I did," Chase responded and then the guilt invaded his face. His green eyes said he loved his little girl, but his stance said he felt remorse for hurting me, but I wasn't sure I cared. "I wanted to tell you."

"Why didn't you? We have all been taking care of her. I held that baby in my arms and loved her like my own even after what you did. What makes you think I wouldn't have forgiven you and raised her with you?"

Chase put his hands in his pockets and started to talk when I finally had something real to say.

"You cheat on me, and then you get shot. Instead of telling anyone, you go off and play command and conquer on whatever you were working on. Then you show up here expecting me to forget the hell I have been through and come home with you."

Chase stood there as I got angrier at him. I couldn't help it. The more I said out loud, the worse my rage got. The pain that I endured trying to move past him was excruciating and yet here he stood, asking me to ignore it.

"Candy," he started and I put my hand up. I walked over and stood in front of him so he had to look me in the eye.

"My name is Candice! Only my friends and family can call me Candy, and you are neither." I was nearly yelling and yet he continued to speak calmly.

"Candice, I know what I have done, but I need to make this right. I want you to be part of Chelle's life and I want you to stop hating me. I need you to remember the good over the bad. I want you to leave New York and start over with me."

"I can't do this with you," I yelled. "I am not in a place where I can discuss this with you calmly right now."

"Candice, I want you to think about this. You wouldn't be this upset if you didn't still have feelings for me," Chase spoke softly.

"I have a feeling for you all right, but it is not one you want me to have."

"I deserve your wrath for as long as you want to dish it. I deserve worse, but I love you, Candy, and I will wait for you until my last dying breath."

I rolled my eyes and was torn somewhere between aggravation and extreme emotional distress. I think I could go on a killing spree and Brooklyn would get the charges dropped as fiery indecision flooded my veins.

"Candice, I love you," Chase whispered and I wiggled my finger to tell him to come closer.

"You really love me?" I asked sweetly. He nodded and I placed my hands on his shoulders. "Would you die for me?" I asked and he nodded. I leaned in slowly, and he closed his eyes as my lips hovered just above his. Just when I could feel his breath over my skin, I quickly lifted my knee and hit him in the groin. "If you are dead, be dead. If not, then no more disappearing acts."

I watched him fall to the floor. He groaned in agony as he cupped his balls. I thought it would make me feel better, but I only felt worse.

"You won't have to wait long for that last dying breath if you don't leave. I think Candice has been through enough," Mark spoke up for me and I actually breathed a sigh of relief that he had.

Chase pulled himself up off the floor, still holding himself, and headed out the door. I felt an immediate weight lift off my shoulders.

"I think you should call Jax and go on your honeymoon," Mark stated and I started to protest when he cut me off. "This is none of my business, but you and Jax need this. You can get separate rooms or whatever you need to do, but staying in town and dealing with that every single day is going to be rough."

"Why do you think it would be every day?" I asked. I thought Chase would move on or wait for me to come to him.

"That man right there is a fighter, and goes after whatever he sets his sights on. Right now what he wants is you."

I knew Mark was right when he put it like that. He acted like my big brother these days and I was suddenly very grateful for Brooklyn's incessant need to be nosy that led her to call me when I was in California.

These people were part of my family now, and while I welcomed their advice here, I didn't want to go. I just wanted to live, breathe, and love without reservation or pain.

"We could go," Brooklyn spoke up. "I can get us there," she stated with a wink for Mark, who looked like he was calculating something in his head.

"I guess we are going on vacation together. This will be so much fun," I said with the fakest cheer I could muster up. Brooklyn read right through my phony enthusiasm and wrapped her arms around me and whispered in my ear.

"Take it one day at a time."

Chapter 3

"I want you to know that just because I am here and I am going on this trip with you doesn't mean anything has changed from how I felt last night. I just need to get out of town for a few days," I spoke softly as I sipped the Tim Horton's coffee that Jax had brought for himself, but gave to me.

"Can I tell you I am glad you are coming?" Jax asked. His eyes danced with delight the second I showed up. He was going to go alone, and here I was invading his trip to run away from my fiancé with my husband. *I sounded like a trailer park reality series.*

"You can and I will reply with I am getting my own room."

Jax smiled and almost looked relieved. I was wearing my heart out for all the world to see. I tried to hide my love for him, but my words couldn't change the way I looked at my husband. He and I both knew I wanted to be angry with him for anything and everything, but I was only furious with myself.

He took the handle of my bag and carried it through the airport for me. We made it through security without an issue and sat at the gate waiting to board our flight when my dad called.

"Hey dad," I answered.

"Candy Cane, how are you holding up?"

"I'm still breathing, dad. I guess that counts for something," I replied in a whisper as I stood up and walked to the wall of windows. I nearly downed the coffee, thanks to a crappy night's sleep

"It does. You have to keep breathing and everything will get better. So, tell me what you are doing," my dad replied.

"Getting ready to board the plane with Jax."

"Oh, thank goodness," my dad said and I was instantly confused.

"Why do you say that?"

"Candy, you avoid conflict like it is the plague. I thought you would leave Jax because Chase showed up as some irrational act or something."

I took a deep breath and turned my head to look at Jax. He was so handsome and he loved me, but so did Chase, or so he said anyway.

"Dad, I am only going on this trip to get away from everything. I gave Jax back his rings last night."

"Candice-Leigh Carson Monroe!" My dad called out my whole name. He was so loud there were people in the airport staring at my phone. "You tell me what Jaxson did to warrant losing his wife! You took vows and they are very serious vows. You wouldn't have spoken them if you didn't mean them."

"Dad, he used me in a bet," I replied with the only plausible excuse I could think of and I swore I heard my father cuss under his breath.

"You will always be my daughter and I will love you no matter how dense you become as you age," my dad said through gritted teeth, as if he was angry.

"Dad!" I yelled into the phone.

"Candy, I swear to God you run from everything that gets complicated. I know it sucks that Chase decided to just pop up, but it doesn't mean that anything has to change."

I took a deep breath and looked back at Jax again. I heard Chelle cry in the background and then I heard Chase's voice as he soothed her.

"Dad it changes everything," I replied in hopes of not making my dad any angrier.

"Why?" My dad asked and I couldn't answer him. "Candy Cane, if Chase had been alive this whole time, would you have stayed with him after learning about Chelle?"

"Probably. I mean, I don't know. I wasn't given the choice."

"Because Chase didn't want you to have the option. He decided for you when he made the decision not to tell you and kept it from you. He made the decision to go undercover when he woke up in the hospital. He never once sat you down and talked to you about what you wanted. He chose to leave you in the most painful form anyone can leave another. I want you happy and I don't believe you will be with Chase."

"Daddy, I can't hurt either one of them," I whispered into the phone and my dad sighed.

"Candy Cane, you have always tried to shelter others, but you can't do that here. I *bet* you are not even mad about this so-called wager. I think you are scared to pick your husband who is better for you because of the history you have with Chase. Your stubbornness gets in the way, but I wholeheartedly believe you are scared of your happily ever after."

"Dad," I spoke softly. "I am not good enough for him."

"What the hell makes you think that?" my dad scoffed.

"I ran. I didn't stand and defend my marriage or Jax. Without a thought, or even a look back at any of them, I fled the scene. I am only going to hurt Jax in the end. Maybe it would be best if I ended it now."

"Candice, don't do anything stupid. You are emotional-."

I hung up on my dad as Jax motioned me over. I tried hard to hide the tears in my eyes and headed to the plane. We went up to first class and sat side by side as there were no other open seats where I could just breathe for a minute.

I leaned my seat into the bed position and laid down. I closed my eyes and decided I was going to just sleep the whole way to Saint Lucia.

"Candice," Jax called my name and I opened my eyes. "I can't imagine how you feel right now but I want you to know if there is a fight for you, my hat is in the ring. I was serious when I took my vows, and for better or worse, in sickness and health, till death do us part, you are stuck with me."

"Jax you can't possibly understand," I whispered as I sat back up.

"Try me," he smiled at me and I turned to face him.

"Seeing him brought it all back. I could see our history and the love we shared. I see the same with you, but I was with him for so long that being with you feels like I am betraying what he and I had. I made a wish to get closure and it failed," I replied softly. "If the water doesn't grant wishes and stars can't, then where do you put your faith? Who do you turn to when you screw up?"

"Candice, maybe him coming back is the closure you need. I happened to think your wishes worked because I wished for you every day." Jax then brushed his thumb across my face and wiped away my tear. "I always knew you were the one, but you were always his. You made a wish in our front yard when I was a fool and nearly let you go; do you remember what you wished for?"

I thought back to that moment when I thought he hated me and the sky opened up just as I was leaving, as if it was as sign to stay. I remember making a wish and running back and kissing him goodbye, only the electricity between us made me think it wasn't over.

"I wished you a happy life," I whispered as he wiped another tear off my face.

"Candy, you are my heaven. You are where I want to be every second of every day. I am happy every moment I am with you. I am content in my life because you are by my side." Jax pulled me over to him and I fell over on his chest as he placed a kiss on top of my head.

"If I stay with you, he gets hurt. If I leave you, you get hurt. No matter what I do someone gets hurt," I softly cried as an unnatural guilt started churning in my gut.

"Candy, stop thinking about what we want. What do you want?" Jax asked and I watched as his heart shattered like humpty dumpty when I whispered those three words that stabbed him.

"I don't know."

Chapter 4

"What do you mean there are no more rooms?" I asked angrily as the concierge explained that they booked up their last room just this morning.

"I'm sorry, Mrs. Monroe, but there are no more rooms."

Jax smiled as I growled and turned to walk ahead of him to my room.

"You can sleep on a couch or in the tub or something, so at least there is a wall between us," I demanded and Jax laughed out loud.

We walked over a bridge and found our room near the water facing Jade Mountain. I opened the door and suddenly realized exactly why he was laughing.

"Where are the walls, doors, and windows?" I exclaimed as the concierge came to hand me my cell phone I left on the desk.

"Here at Jade Mountain there are no walls, windows, or electronics, like televisions and phones. We want you to relax and enjoy your romantic get-a-way."

I turned and glared through him as I snatched my phone back. He ran off muttering something about booking me a massage as soon as possible.

"Candy, do you remember when I said I wanted to take you to a place where we could do everything naked, and you laughed and said okay," Jax started to explain as we entered the room and closed the door. "I found a place that does just that."

He smiled like he had just climbed Mount Everest without breaking a sweat. His cheek dimples and bedroom eyes were definitely screaming at me to swoon over him.

"We can just book a new flight home, and leave tomorrow."

Then Jax held up his phone, and shook his head with a sly grin.

Fuck, no electronics.

I walked further into the room and gasped when I saw the view. The four poster canopy bed was screened in and faced the edge of the mountain and the ocean that surrounded it. Not five feet from the bed was a quarter wall that held back the water from the pool in the room. I stepped closer and followed the stream to see the pool led out into the ocean. There was a beautiful beach just a short walkway away.

"The view is breathtaking," I spoke up as I let go of my anger and walked to the edge of the room where water surrounded us.

"It truly is," Jax said and I turned to see he was talking about me. I felt my cheeks heat up in a crimson blush and I turned my back to him to hide my involuntary smile.

"Maybe we should change clothes and go get some food," I stated, turning around just in time to catch Jax throwing all of our clothes in the hot tub.

"What the hell are you doing?" I screamed.

"Honeymooning," Jax said with a sly grin. That was the moment I found the bathroom and saw there was no door or wall to hide the toilet.

"Oh, hell no," I shouted as Jax looked to the corner of the room and laughed. "You are going to have to leave the room every time I need to pee or shower or change or-,"

Jax walked over and placed his finger on my lips to quiet me. I immediately shut up as I relished the way his skin felt against mine. He stepped closer till we were chest to chest.

Jax then leaned down and placed his silky lips on mine and gave me the most insatiable kiss ever. My hands involuntarily went to his hips as he wrapped his hands around my neck and brushed his tongue against my lips.

I opened to him as if I had been trained to do so on command. His flavor invaded my core while I let out a moan that he swallowed down. He moved his hands down and pushed my back till I was flush against him.

I placed my hands on his hardened chest and pushed away as the blood in my body flooded to my clit, pulsing with a dire need to have my husband.

"I can't right now," I whispered and Jax placed his hand under my chin, gently forcing me to look at him.

"I won't pretend I understand it, but I will wait as long as you need me to."

"Do you want to see if Brooklyn and Mark checked in yet?" I asked as I put distance between us and slowed my breathing.

"Why would they be here?" Jax asked, confusion plastered across his face and in his tone as he crossed his arms.

"They decided to come out as well," I spoke softly.

"This is our honeymoon. I don't want that serial killer drama here. What if something happens to you?" Jax asked as he started to pace.

"What are you talking about?" I replied and he turned and gave me a sultry smile.

"That is for another book. Right now I want to work on our story," he stated as he stopped pacing to kiss me lightly.

"What are we going to do now that all our clothes are wet?" I asked, placing my hands on my hips.

"Are you tired? Hungry? Dirty? Bored?" Jax asked.

"No, no, no, and no," I replied as his dimples screamed for me to just let go of the hurt I felt from the wedding.

"And the sex is out, right?" He asked and I giggled as I nodded my head.

"How about a massage?"

"Okay, but you are not giving it to me. You and I both know where it will lead," I replied.

"Killjoy," Jax retorted as he turned his back and I laughed. No matter what was happening around us, I knew Jax could make me giggle like a school girl while I blushed a rainbow of pinks and reds across my face.

"Hey Jax." He turned to look at me. "I got a finger for you." He cocked his eyebrow with intrigue. "But you are not going to like it." Then I shot him my middle finger.

He prowled toward me and I took a few steps back. I was between Jax and a quarter-wall holding back water. I stood my ground as he got closer. He took my hand and grabbed my middle finger, sucking it into his mouth.

"You don't play fair," I whimpered as my hormones danced with need and sped up my heart.

"Nothing is fair in love, war, and sex," he spoke with a silvery tone as he pulled my finger out of his mouth.

"Jax, this isn't fair," I mouthed as I placed my head on his chest.

"Damn it, Candice. I am trying really hard to understand how you feel and be sympathetic, but I am just like you. My best friend just returned from the dead to take my wife and ride off into the sunset, but I am not letting that get between you and I because he chose his life without us, and I chose mine with you."

"Jax, you are nothing like me. I spent over twenty years with Chase. I belonged to him for two decades and I have only been with you like this a little over a year. My heart is broken because, while I love you more than anything else, my head says I am cheating on Chase by being with you. It's hard to breathe around you because it feels like us being together is wrong."

Then Jax turned and left the room, leaving me all alone, when I needed him the most. He was giving me the space I didn't want, but had been asking for all along.

Chapter 5

"Wake up, Candy," Jax whispered and I pulled the blanket over my head. "Candy Cane," he called out as a sing-song. "Come on Candice."

"I changed my name to mud between the hours of midnight and six. If it is between those hours, go outside and find me."

"Too late, I already found my mud, and it is time for you to get up. We are headed out for a while. I have an itinerary," Jax spoke up and I pulled the blanket down to look at him shuffling papers that had a massive list of things to do on it.

"Nope," I replied and pulled the blanket back up over me. I felt him get up off the bed, but I knew it was far from over.

"Oh you are going and you are going to have fun," Jax challenged and I murmured the word 'no' as I hid from the early morning sunlight. "Candice, if you don't go, I am pouring your Tim Horton's into the toilet."

I immediately pulled the blanket down again and saw my hot pink travel coffee mug that read 'should be reading' across the front.

"Is that really Timmy's?" I asked and he smirked.

"Yes it is. I snuck it in and paid off the concierge to make sure you had it every morning, but I only brought enough for one cup a day," Jax chuckled as he let the cup slide further down his hand.

I threw off the blanket and leapt out of bed to take the cup from him. Then I turned and climbed back into the bed, pulling the blanket over me.

"You are the worst at getting up in the morning," Jax spoke up.

"You should be arrested for almost putting my coffee in the toilet," I replied and Jax laughed. "You premeditated an attempt to murder my coffee. I should arrest you! That is a crime!"

"That is not a crime, and you let me do the arresting. I will let you sleep in till 7AM tomorrow," Jax offered, but I knew him well enough to know better. He was always up early and I was up late writing my books while he slept.

"What do you have me doing today?" I asked with a groan as I sat up on the bed, and sipped my coffee.

"Me," Jax cocked an eyebrow with his half – smile and I shook my head at him. He seemed disappointed, but moved on without saying anything. "First, we are going to breakfast, then shopping, and after lunch, we are going to go swimming with the sharks-,"

"No nope nada nuh uh and did I mention hell no," I replied, cutting him off. "There will be no reenactment of Jaws anywhere near me.

"Candy that was a movie," Jax spoke softly as he walked over to the bed.

"Movies are based on real life," I replied and he smirked.

"Movies are based on what is inside someone's head."

"No sharks!" I nearly yelled trying to get my freak out under control. "I can see the headlines now, 'Candice Monroe eaten by a shark when she didn't give it up to her husband on their honeymoon.' Everyone would call it an act of karma." Jax burst out laughing.

"I think you are blowing it out of proportion, but we can do something else."

Two hours later, I was laying on my stomach on the beach reading a book on my kindle that Jax had snuck in for me when a shadow casted over me.

"Hey honey," I stated with a smile as Jax stood above me.

"Hey gorgeous, come take a swim with me," Jax pleaded, as he dropped water all over me. I looked up at him; the sun glistened over every muscle that rippled across him. He ran his hand through his wet hair to give me the view of his chiseled-by-the-Gods face, and ravishing grey eyes.

God, my husband was sexy.

"No, I am reading," I whined and he reached down and took my kindle. "Hey, that is grounds for divorce," I shouted and he read over the first paragraph on the page I was on.

"I am better than this book boyfriend of yours," Jax stated as he walked toward the ocean with my kindle barely being held in his fingers.

I jumped to my feet and ran for him. He laughed as we ran circles around each other.

"You are meaner than a book boyfriend," I chastised.

"Only because you love it," Jax replied and I ran straight for him. He threw my Kindle near my towel and picked me up around my waist, carrying me into the ocean as I squealed.

"Jax," I warned, but once he was far enough out, he dropped me into the warm salty water and I had to swim back up. "Jax I can't touch the bottom," I shouted and he laughed.

"Short people problems," he murmured as he pulled me to him.

"Better to be a short person and be able to hide than to be a beacon for all to see," I replied and he merely shook his head as I wrapped my legs around his waist.

I leaned back and allowed my upper body to float on the water as my legs stayed wrapped around Jax.

"I love you, Candy. I don't think I would be half the man I am without you by my side and in my arms."

I could hear Jax professing his feelings for me, but I ignored it as though the water was in my ears. I didn't know what to say. Everything in my life felt like a movie clip where the speeches didn't line up with the lip movement.

I felt the side strings on my white bikini give way and soon I saw the fabric in Jax's hand.

"Jax," I warned as I pulled myself up to him. I didn't want to tell him no. I didn't want to hurt anyone, but something was very wrong with the way my head was working.

"Candice, I want to make love to my wife in the ocean on our honeymoon," Jax whispered before he kissed my neck. I gripped his shoulders as my brain and my body did a tug of war over what I would allow.

Jax kissed my neck as I gripped his hair and groaned. I felt his hardened length at my entrance when the sun glistened and I thought I saw Chase on the beach. I shuddered and pushed Jax back. Jax looked concerned as I quivered, but when I looked back at our private beach, there was no one there.

"Jax, I want to, but," I started and Jax pulled my body away from his far enough to put my bottoms back on. He fixed his white swim trunks. Then he carried me out of the ocean.

We didn't speak about it again as the day went onward. We played volleyball and horseshoes on the social beach with other guests. We were getting ready to go get dinner when I thought about doing something special for him since he was being patient with me.

I wore my bikini with a sarong I'd purchased in the hotel shop as we sent our hot tub soaked clothes to be laundered.

Jax held out his hand to me and I took it. I felt like a scolded child and kept my lips shut even though I had done nothing wrong. I mean, it is my body, my choice, yet I felt like I just drove a wedge between us.

Jax took me down the wood paneled corridor until it opened up into yet another room with no walls or windows. Tables lined the water's edge all the way around.

I noticed white tiled floor covered in rose petals that made the shapes of arrows leading the way as we walked in, and candles flourished the room as the fire danced to the wind. There were no other guests here but us.

We moved through the tables as a violinist came up behind us and started playing a rendition of *"See You Again"* by *Wiz Khalifa*. A pianist joined in as Jax led me to the middle of the room and pulled me into his arms.

I molded my body to his as he placed my hand in his and his other arm wrapped around my back and we danced to the music.

"What are you doing?" I whispered as all the employees rushed to get our dinner table set up.

"I never got to have the first dance with my wife," Jax spoke softly and I laid my head on his hardened chest to hear the beats of a heart that called my name.

Jax reached into the pocket of his swim shorts and pulled out my rings. He then took my hand and put my rings back on my finger.

"No matter what is happening around us that makes us sad, or freaks us out, we have each other for life, and these rings represent more than marriage. By wearing these, I know you love me, but more importantly, I know that you are my best friend," Jax whispered. I laid on his chest and stared at the rings as tears welled up in my eyes and I started to cry.

"Why are you crying?" Jax asked and I sniffled in a very unladylike manner.

"Because you are perfect," I sobbed as everything came to a peak.

"Isn't that a good thing?" Jax asked, forcing me to look at him.

"I am not good enough for you. I will continue hurting you." I pulled away and ran a hand through my ombre'd hair as hysteria started to set in. "Fuck, Jax I love you," I cried.

"Candy," Jax started, and I cut him off.

"The scariest part of my life was letting him go, and I didn't know it till I saw him, but I still love him. Now the thing that I am most afraid of is hurting you because some part of my heart wants him," I replied, and took off running to the beach.

There was no lighthouse and no storm. There was no sun to shine down on me and give me warmth. I felt cold and alone.

I walked into the ocean and just dropped like a rock. I felt the water crash over every part of me and just went with it. As the waves knocked me to and fro, I sympathized with the constant barrage that the waves underwent from the winds.

Hands grabbed me and I fought to stay in my water. I wanted to beg and plead to whoever would listen to take these choices away from me. I wanted to heal, but Chase showing up had torn me back open as if I hadn't moved forward at all in the last year. Him being alive made me feel like a traitor because I had married his best friend.

"Candy," Jax called out as I continued to fight to stay in the water. "Candy, stop," he stated as he pulled me into his arms and I sobbed.

"I don't want to hurt you," I cried.

"I am a big boy, sweetheart. Let me make the decision on when I have had enough."

"I feel so guilty about falling in love with you and that is not fair. You make me happy Jax, so why aren't I happy?" I replied and Jax held me tighter.

"It will be all right. I promise you we will get through this," Jax whispered in my ear as he picked me up like a bride and carried me back to the hotel.

As we got into the room, Jax pulled off our wet clothes and pulled me into the bed. I could feel his cock harden behind me and wanted to have him, but my heart said it would complicate things.

I wiggled to put space between us, but he merely held me tighter.

"Candy," Jax whispered in my ear. "I am not going to push you, but can I have a good to go with the bad kiss."

I turned to look at my gorgeous husband whose grey eyes lit up as soon as I faced him. This man loved me more than I loved myself.

As I placed my lips on his, I had to wonder, was I throwing everything away? Would being with him ever stop feeling like betrayal?

"Jax," I whispered when he pulled back to look at me. "Can you hold me tight all night?" I asked and he pushed my wet hair off my face. He placed a light kiss to my lips.

"I will do anything you want me to as long as you want me here."

I felt a sudden wave of guilt. Chase had hurt me, and I hurt Jax. History was repeating itself, and I was going to lose them both all over again.

"Candice, just give me a chance to be your husband and I promise I won't let you regret your choice."

"Promise me something," I whispered against his chest.

"Anything," he replied.

"Promise me that when I break like this that, I can do so in your arms. I want your word that even if we hate each other, when I crumble, you will catch me in your arms and hold me together until the glue sets me right again."

"I promise Candy. I won't ever let go."

Chapter 6

"Wake up, Candy," Jax called out and I cracked an eyelid to see it was the next day.

"No," I pouted and he laughed.

"I will tickle you till you get out of bed," Jax whispered and I groaned at him. "I will throw you in the water," he warned, and I pulled the blanket up over my head.

I felt myself being lifted and I grabbed onto him. If I was going in the water, so was he.

"If I get wet, you are sleeping in the doghouse for the rest of your life," I growled.

"As long as it is our doghouse, I am good with it."

"Jax, I just want to sleep," I whimpered and felt him lay me back on the bed.

"You are the worst at getting up," Jax chuckled and I squeezed my eyes shut tightly. "Come on. They brought breakfast and you have a solo massage scheduled this afternoon."

"Ugh, fine," I groaned and rolled over to see my handsome husband smiling down on me as the sun crested over the mountains.

I reached up and pulled his face down to mine and he placed his lips on mine. I felt like we were falling in love all over again, as we worked to overcome my setback. He was being patient, and I couldn't imagine Chase being that way, but then again, I didn't know Chase anymore.

"Good morning," Jax whispered as I let him go and he placed another kiss on my forehead.

"Our clothes should be back sometime today. Mark and Brooklyn got in last night and we are going to head into town and give you some time alone. I want to get you a wedding present."

I got up and put on the robe that Jax had laid out for me, and we ate the beautiful breakfast spread that he had ordered. He even had my Tim

Horton's coffee ready because he knew I was slightly obsessed with their coffee.

"I have a surprise for you before I go," Jax spoke softly as I watched him change into clothes from the hotel gift shop that had such bright colors I couldn't look directly at it.

"What is it?" I asked as I impatiently waited to see what it was. Then I watched as he pulled my iPad from his day-pack bag.

"I was hoping this trip might be memorable enough that you would want to write about it," he smiled and walked over to me.

I took the iPad from him and lightly tossed it to the bed as I wrapped my hand behind his neck and forced his lips to mine.

He pulled me tightly to him and I moaned as his tongue slipped into my mouth. My body trembled with unreleased tension as Jax pulled away breathlessly.

"What was that for?" He asked without pushing me for more.

"I wanted to say thank you," I replied with a smug smile. A knock on the door sounded and Jax released me and adjusted himself.

"When I get back, I am going to tell you you're welcome my way," he stated with a wink and walked out to head into town with Mark and Brooklyn.

I took a shower, and made some notes on a book I had started working on as the hours seemed to pass by in the blink of an eye. Happened a lot when I got lost in a story. Before I knew it, there was a knock on the door.

"Hello," a male voice called into the room.

"Hi, are you the masseuse?" I asked, and the elderly man nodded as he brought in his table. He set it up and placed a sheet down. He brought in heated oils on a cart and plugged them up.

"I will be ready in five minutes if you want to get undressed and cover with the sheet, I will be back," he spoke softly and I nodded.

I took off my robe and laid it on the bed, then I walked over and climbed up on the table. I closed my eyes as I listened to the waves crash along the beach. This place really was heaven. I needed to start enjoying it.

I heard my door open and shut and then I heard him grab the oil. I felt him pour warm baby oil type lotion on my back and then he proceeded to rub my shoulders.

I groaned as he worked the knot out of my neck, but I could feel my tension return as he worked. As soon as he worked one knot out there were four more would tense up all over my body. I had to relax. I let my mind drift to the one thing that was bothering me.

I could still feel a pull to Chase and didn't understand why. Could it be because we had known each other so long? Could it be because we were once intimate? Could it be fate telling me I was with the wrong man?

I knew Jax had done nothing wrong. I knew that I should be so furious with Chase that I never spoke to him again. But some part of me cared about him enough that I didn't want to hurt him no matter how badly he had hurt me. Two wrongs never made a right.

I was getting ready to warn the masseuse that I was ticklish on the hip bone, but he avoided it, and I tried to relax again. He pulled the sheet up over my butt as he went to work on my legs, which were as tense as my shoulders, it seemed. Maybe I wasn't the type to enjoy a massage from a stranger because his touch was keeping me on edge.

I tried to focus in on the sound of the waves, which wasn't hard, as they were growing bigger with the sound of an incoming storm off the horizon. I thought about making a wish on the water for Chase, but what would be the point when no one listened.

I felt a tap and turned to roll over, re-adjusting the sheet as I closed my eyes and listened to the invigorating sound of the storm. It sounded so angry that I opened my eyes and looked to see there was no storm on the horizon. Confusion set in, as I turned my head toward the sound and gasped.

"What are you doing here?" I asked Chase who was dressed as an employee.

"Making you fall in love with me again," he whispered as I pulled the sheet around me and climbed off the table. I kicked the iPod dock on the bottom of the cart that was playing my storm and wanted to slam a door, but there were none.

"Chase, you need to leave," I spoke angrily, feeling like my privacy had been invaded.

"Give me an hour, Candy, please," he begged and while I wanted to tell him to stop calling me Candy, I let it go, took a deep breath, and nodded my head. I was going to have to get him out of my system one way or another.

I spun my finger to tell him to turn around and he did while I put on my robe.

"You look like you have been working out," Chase pointed out.

"That is what happens when you run from killers, and have to beat up your ex's baby momma," I stated sarcastically as he turned back around.

"I heard about it all, but I didn't know until it started going down or I would have been there sooner."

"Sooner?" I asked, but as soon as the words left my lips, I remembered Vanessa's story about a man who came out of nowhere and killed Andrew and his men.

"You were there in the house that night? And on the street when I was at the Cafeteria? You were there at the light house?" I asked as I walked over to the bed in disbelief. I had thought seeing him and hearing him had been a sign from God, but instead it was because he was lurking in the shadows.

"I was there, Candy. I have always been nearby. I couldn't let you go like that. I had to stay close." He spoke softly as he took a seat in the living room chair that was right across from the bed.

"You were there to drive me insane, thinking I couldn't move on. I mean, you couldn't take sixty seconds and tell me you were alive?"

"Candice, you don't understand. I couldn't."

"Your letter," I whispered. He walked over and sat on the bed beside me, taking my hands in his when I started to cry, remembering the dead man's words.

"I meant every word," he said as tears streamed down my face. "I loved you so much, but it was easier to be dead."

"The body in the coffin?" I asked and he wiped the tears and pulled me into his arms.

"That was me. Illusions and medical science make anything believable."

I sobbed into my hands as my brain reminded me of how hard it was to see him in his uniform and know that he had taken my heart with him. I remember all the tears that were shed and the way Jax tried to be strong, but blamed himself.

"Why did you decide this without me?" I asked, and then came the answer I already knew was coming.

"Because you deserved better than what I had done."

I shook my head and tried to halt my tears, but there was something so very emotional when it came to my feelings for Chase.

"You are a moron, and I don't believe that answer for a minute. Christina told me what happened and I wasn't overly mad you cheated. I know you did it to save her life," I spoke, almost silently.

"Candy, I am so sorry I hurt you like that. It nearly killed me as I watched from the sidelines as you fell in love with my best friend and brother. Watching you with someone else was so hard that I can't even imagine how I would feel if you had a baby with him and had to see the evidence of it every day."

"What are you going to do about Chelle?" I asked and he smiled when I mentioned her name.

"I am not going to get in the way of the family our parents have created for her. Right now, I just want to get to know her. Watch over her like a guardian angel."

I leaned my head over onto Chase's shoulder and enjoyed the familiarity of having him there. I had missed him every day for so long that I couldn't trust my feelings for him. I wanted this man to be the Chase I remembered before my heart shattered and healed. I wanted to feel that way again, but I didn't.

"I do love you, Candy Cane, and that won't change no matter how much you hate me."

I turned and looked into those green eyes I knew so well. I could see memories of us as kids playing at the park, hand holding, and football practices. Stolen kisses under bleachers and the magical night he took my virginity. I saw him when he tried to shoulder the pain from losing my mom. I saw my life in his eyes.

"I don't hate you, Chase," I whispered as I laid back on the bed with an exacerbated sigh. "In the last few days, I have envisioned ripping your nuts off, cutting your heart out with a spoon, tying you up in a closet and forcing you to watch me live happily ever after, or just walking away from you, but that is because I am angry. Not because I hate you."

"Can I ask you how exactly it happened with Jax? I saw it happen, but I want to know the moment you knew," Chase asked and I turned my head to look over at him as he held my gaze.

"One night we were laying in the bed together like we used to do when we went camping." I smiled and Chase cut me off.

"You mean, when I went camping and you hid in the tent from bugs," he smiled.

"Yeah, we were bundled up just like that and everything came to a point where everything was out of my control. I just let go, and Jax was there in a different light."

"Did you want him or did you miss me?" Chase asked and that was a loaded question that I really didn't want to answer. I sat back up and turned to look at him while I thought about what to say.

"I wanted him. I was trying like hell to move on from you. I can never replace what you and I had, but I found myself in Jax in a way I never saw myself with you. At first I thought it was loneliness, and ran, but when I got to California, I knew I loved him, but you already knew how I felt."

"I knew. I saw it coming a long time before it did," Chase spoke softly as he brushed his hand across my cheek.

"Why did Andrew come for me and Jax?" I asked. It had always bothered me as to why I was involved.

"Andrew placed himself near you to see if I would show because he believed I was alive," Chase whispered as he brushed my brown and blond ombre'd hair behind my ear.

"Did you miss me, Candy?" Chase asked and I nodded my head. "Then what are you doing here with him? Come away with me."

"Chase." I let out a sigh as I toyed with my fingers. "He was there when you left me all alone. He knows me better than I know myself sometimes and he never left me. He loves me."

"I love you," Chase whispered as he leaned over and placed his lips on mine. As warm tingles covered my flesh, I pushed him back and let a tear fall.

"You need to go," I whispered.

"I am everywhere, Candy. If you ever need me, just yell. I will only come running for you," Chase sighed and then he walked out of the room.

Chapter 7

"Hey, Candy," Jax called as he entered the room with a large gift box.

"We need to talk," I replied and his smile fell.

"Open this first," Jax said and I walked over and took the heavy box that was covered in white wrapping paper and a large pink bow.

I sat it on the bed and pulled the bow strings, letting it fall open as Jax started putting new clothes in a dresser for us. I tore the white paper and then pried the top of the box open as the tape tried to hold me back.

My hands went to my mouth as I gasped at what sat in the box. Jax walked up behind me and wrapped his arms around my waist as I turned into him and began to cry.

"Did I do something wrong?" He asked and I shook my head. "Do you like it?" He questioned and I nodded. I turned in his arms and pulled out a typewriter.

This wasn't just any typewriter. It was a Smith-Premier No. 1 typewriter circa 1889. It had nickel decorative plates and two keyboards, one for lower case and one for capitals. It was a blind-writer; you couldn't see what you were writing until you moved two lines down.

I was completely overwhelmed that he had found one for me. They cost thousands of dollars, which is why I had never been able to get one.

"This is just like the one my mom had," I whispered as memories flooded me of her teaching me to type on it. Her grandmother had given her the one we had. We used it every day while she taught me how to make stories. She made me the author I was today by sitting in front of one of these.

"I don't remember what happened to your mom's, but since I hadn't gotten you a wedding present, I thought that this was appropriate," Jax explained and I sat the typewriter down carefully.

"It was stolen. A few years after she died, before we moved into the cape cod house outside the city. It had been stolen, along with her pearls."

Jax held me tighter as my emotional well was filling up. I ran my finger across the white and black keys. I pressed one down and it actually worked. I cried into my hands.

"Candy, these are not happy tears. What's wrong? What did we need to talk about?"

"I'm falling, Jax. I need you to be my glue," I spoke softly as I turned and wrapped my arms around Jax, reveling in the warmth that always exuded from him. When I was finally able to reign in my tears, I took a step back out of his grasp.

"I'm here, Candy Cane. Just tell me how to help and I will," Jax replied as he held me tight.

"Chase was here while you were gone," I whispered. Jax let go and walked over to sit in the chair at the dining table. I could see the pain in his eyes, but I couldn't keep a secret like this from him.

"What happened, Candice? How did he know where to find you?" Jax used my name and not my nick name, which told me more about how he felt than what his face was showing.

"I don't know how he found me. He was the masseuse, or pretended to be. I didn't know it was him at first, but something about his touch kept me on edge. I didn't know it was him until I looked up and saw him," I spoke quietly as tears fell from my eyes. I watched as Jax's face turned from angry to murderous.

"He touched you!" Jax growled as he stood up and began to pace. I held my hand up to tell him there was more. He froze as his arms crossed and his jaw clinched with the teeth he was grinding to hold in his anger.

"We kissed," I explained, but Jax knew what I had said even if I didn't make a sound. Jax turned into a statue. He didn't yell or storm out. He never said he hated me or anything else that I had conjured inside my head.

"Say something!" I screamed as the extended uncommunicative silence gutted me.

"What do you want me to say? Do you want me to ask why you would let him kiss you, but you push me away when I try to be with you? Do you want me to ask if you are considering leaving me for him?" Jax asked and he walked over and placed his hand under my chin, forcing me to look at him as tears flowed down my face. Then he placed his

soft lips on my tear stained cheek and gave me a kiss. "I need some air," he whispered. Then he turned on his heel and walked out the door.

"Candy," a voice shouted before I heard knocking on the door as it echoed through the room. I crawled out of bed and turned to see that my husband didn't come back to the room last night.

I wiped my exhausted eyes and opened the door to a hyper and bouncy Brooklyn. She was standing there with my coffee mug full of steaming coffee, and a smile.

She was wearing a two-piece cobalt bikini that matched her eyes and a sheer black sarong that matched her hair. No matter what we were doing, she found a way to match and yet I was lucky if my bra and panties matched.

"How did you get my coffee mug?" I asked as I tried to wake up enough to be aware of my surroundings.

"Your husband asked me to get your coffee from the concierge while he and Mark got the boat ready. Didn't he tell you?"

I shook my head and invited her in while I explained about Chase and dressed in my white bikini and white sarong. I put on a big floppy hat and huge sunglasses to hide how I was feeling.

"That explains the change in his itinerary. We are going out on a boat he rented this morning. Won't be back till tomorrow night." Brooklyn verbalized his plans as if she was thinking out loud.

"What am I going to do?" I asked. Brooklyn set down her own coffee mug and walked over, pulling my sunglasses down to expose my red rimmed blue eyes.

"Did you kiss Chase back?" She asked inquisitively.

"I don't know it was a kiss."

"Did he pull the thoughts from your mind and send you to that awesome place where it is just you and him? Or were you thinking of Jax when his lips were on yours?" Brooklyn asked and I had to think about it.

"I was thinking that everything was happening really fast and I thought about how much that one kiss would hurt Jax when I pushed him away," I whispered and hoped it was the truth. I knew I had the thoughts after, but the kiss was so fast I don't know if I was thinking or not, but the only place I went was down memory lane with him. There was no euphoric place like with Jax's kiss.

"Okay, how has the sex with Jax been since Chase showed up?" Brooklyn asked and I internally flinched. I knew she was trying to be a friend, but I felt embarrassed about not having my husband on our honeymoon.

"We haven't," I murmured. Brooklyn placed my sunglasses back on my face, and took my hand over to the quarter wall in the room. She pointed out at a cabin ship sitting in the port where Mark and Jax were working diligently to get her ready to set sail.

"Look at your husband out there. Can you tell me that you don't want that delicious piece of NYPD beefcake?" Brooklyn asked and I blushed thirty shades of crimson.

"Of course I want my husband," I replied as embarrassment took over. I wasn't sure why I was reacting like a virgin, but talking about this with Brooklyn just harbored a lot of trust issues. I knew she wasn't Christina, but then again, I never expected Christina to betray me either.

"Girl, listen to me," Brooklyn spoke up as she turned me to face her. "Go get laid, you will feel better." I shook my head as tears filled my eyes.

"What if I call out Chase's name again?"

"Look at it this way, if you are meant to be with Jax, then things will just flow with no hesitation. If you are meant to be with Chase, then you will halt what is happening with your husband."

"What happens if I hesitate with both of them?" I asked, because I had.

"I don't know, Candy, but you need to figure it out. You are stuck in limbo until you do."

"How did you know that Mark was the one for you?" I asked, hopeful that her answer would set me on the right course.

"Remember what I told you in the back of the cab before the shooting and the storm? Before we determined who was good and who was evil?" Brooklyn asked and I nodded, even though I was pretty amped up then and could only remember bits and pieces.

"I asked you if you loved him. When you said yes, I asked you if you could envision your life without him. You have already seen a life without Chase in it and you found your happiness in Jax. Now, can you envision a life without Jax in it?"

Chapter 8

Brooklyn and I spent the next few hours making them wait as we packed. It was amazing just having some girl time with Brooklyn.

After lunch we grabbed our towels and overnight bags and headed toward the ship. I have never been on a boat this size. It was covered in cherry oak embellishments which contrasted the white everywhere else.

I followed Brooklyn below deck and walked down a tiny white corridor until the left side opened up into a kitchen. It had a small refrigerator, and a stove. There were wooden cabinets all along the wall. Brooklyn set down a wooden crate of mixed drinks on the counter and then smiled.

A few feet down was a living room type area with port holes to look out at the water and a bench L-shaped couch that lined the wall. It was red and beige, and covered with pillows.

Then the ship split where there was a cherry oak door on the left and one on the right. Brooklyn went right and then pointed for me to go left. I opened the door to a large bedroom. This was much bigger than I ever envisioned being in a boat. I set my bag down and looked around the room.

A large cherry oak four poster bed sat in the middle of the room, and was garnished in white sheets and a navy blue comforter. I saw fresh flowers on the night stands and there was a porthole just above the small headboard.

There was a door on the right that held a closet. I saw that there was a black dress inside waiting for me with a blue ribbon attached to the hanger and a note.

"Put me on and prepare to sail away with me."

I pulled the dress out and laid it on the bed. Then I opened the door right beside the closet and it opened up into a joint bathroom. There was a shower and toilet, but there was also a door that led into Brooklyn's room.

I closed the bathroom door and turned back to the dress lying on the bed. I felt like I needed to talk to Jax about what had happened, but didn't want to ruin the trip for Brooklyn and Mark. I donned the dress that fit like a glove.

The strapless black sweetheart dress had an empire waistline and allowed the bottom portion of the dress to flow with every twirl. It was so simple, yet made me feel so radiant. I found a mirror on the wall and fixed my hair, and applied minimal make up.

A knock sounded on my door and I opened it to see Mark. He was definitely not who I was expecting.

"Hey Mark, what's up?" I asked and he looked me over from head to toe.

"This is embarrassing. The dress you are wearing was for Brooklyn. I thought she would take this room."

I stood frozen like a deer in headlights. What was I supposed to say? Was I supposed to take off the dress and hand it over? I really wasn't sure what the etiquette was in a situation like this.

"Oh – um," I started to babble when Mark cut me off.

"Candice, you look phenomenal in it so why don't you keep it. It will be our little secret. Go up and show your husband. He is at the helm."

"I'm nervous," I whispered my thoughts out loud and Mark nodded his head. He turned to walk away when something seemed to make him halt his movements.

"Candice, it is none of my business, but walls are thin and voices carry everywhere," Mark stated as he turned to look at me. I tilted my head as questions began to form on my lips.

"I know you have been struggling to know who to be with, who to hurt, and withholding from your husband because you are afraid."

I went to stop him and raised my hand when he took it in his and shushed me.

"Like I said, this is none of my business, but as your adopted vacation buddy, I want to say this before you throw away something real and good. I want you to think about this: When you ran away, who came for you? When your heart broke, who was there to help you heal? When you needed to know love once more, who took you in with open arms?"

I didn't say anything as Mark let go of my hand and started to walk away, when he had one last thing to weigh down on me.

"I guarantee that the person whose name comes to mind when I ask you all that is not the one who ran away from you. It is not the one who caused your heart break. It is not the one who has reappeared. It is not the one you will call out around your husband. Give Jax a break. He is really trying to hold on to what he has with you."

Mark then turned and walked into his room. I took a deep breath and started out the door and down the tiny corridor. I was walking really slow as Mark had planted a seed in my head and I was trying to see it bloom roses. I was near the stairs when Brooklyn came running up and wrapped her arms around me and gave me a hug.

"My dress looks awesome on you. I am so glad I decided not to take that room," she whispered in my ear. I pulled back in question, only for her to display a huge grin. "Nothing I do is ever by accident. Now go show your husband what he is missing by staying angry, and stop being a prude." Then she winked and ran back to her room. I loved that woman when she was out of the office.

I swallowed hard and turned and walked up the stairs, heading across the deck until I saw Jax. I froze as he fiddled with the instruments around him and wondered if I would be turned away.

His eyes met mine and I watched him drink me in as the wind blew my ombre'd hair to the side and the dress flowed with it. I let out a deep breath I had been holding and walked forward slowly.

It seemed like months passed in between each step and my confidence was nonexistent by the time I got close to him. Silence would be my enemy if he said nothing once I stood in front of him.

The wind shifted and my dress blew up and showed him my bikini under it. I didn't bother to pull a Marilyn Monroe and push the dress down. He was my husband and I had no reason to shy away from what he had already seen and where he had already been. At least that is what I told myself to keep my freak out under control.

"You look beautiful," Jax spoke softly as he took my hand and brought my knuckles up to his lips. He laid a soft kiss on them and then pulled me over to face the helm, with him right behind me. I felt his hands go to my waist and his breath caress my ear as he whispered the words, "drive us away from here."

I had no idea what I was doing, but I turned the wheel and then Jax's hand came down over mine and showed me where the power was. We went from the slow turtle to rapid rabbit as we sped away from the resort and out into the ocean.

There was something empowering about controlling a ship that large. I found my confidence and a smidgen of faith that all would be alright as tiny water drops splashed us. I let myself relax and thought the world would be right as rain again, until Jax spoke.

"I am a little calmer now. Do you want to talk about what happened with you and Chase?"

My bubble was officially busted. I lowered the lever and took us to a slower speed and turned to face him as his hands reached around me to control the wheel.

"No, why do you?" I asked with disdain, letting him know that I was moving past it and didn't want to discuss another man with him.

"I don't like him following us here, and then approaching you when I am not around. I trust you completely, but-."

I felt like I was the kid in class wearing the dunce cap. I was only thinking about what I wanted and how I felt. I never took into consideration how Jax felt and that made me the worst wife ever. Even worse, I wasn't even trying to be Jax's friend.

"A year ago, you gripped your steering wheel like you were choking the life out of it when you thought about having a new partner. He is here, and I know he has a lot to answer for, but I think he genuinely wants to be in our lives," I spoke softly.

"Is that what he told you because he hasn't bothered to talk to me about it."

"I want to listen, if you want to talk about it," I whispered and after a few minutes of silence, he turned the ship off and let her coast on the rapid waves. His grey eyes showed me a pain I had never seen before, and I wanted to take him in my arms and comfort him. I needed to ease his pain.

"Chase died. He was my brother and he chose to leave me as family, as his partner, and his best friend. He came back to take my wife away from me and family doesn't do that to each other. So, to me Chase is still dead and this imposter is trespassing on what we have built. I feel like I am losing you to him every single time you turn me away. I think you have already left me because you don't tell me what is going on. I love you Candice, but if you don't start giving me an inch, our marriage is never going to work."

I let out the breath I had been holding and knew he was telling the truth. I had known I was driving a wedge between us and I had kept it there. What I never thought about was how Jax felt about Chase's return. I had never really bothered to ask.

I took Jax's hand and led him below deck and into our quarters. I turned to him and placed a kiss on his rippled abs, whispering the word 'mine.' Then I grabbed his hand and kissed his palm and murmured the same. I placed kisses everywhere I could and told him over and over again how he belonged to me.

I grabbed a pillow from the bed and dropped it onto the floor. I dropped to my knees in front of him and untied his white swim trunks. Then I pulled them down until his hardened cock sprang free as it sat near my lips. I reached my tongue out and licked the head before placing a kiss on the crown and telling him it was mine.

"You have been denying me since we got married. Why now? What are you trying to prove?

Or do you want me because you didn't have Chase yesterday? This isn't one of your books. You don't get to have us both!" Jax growled and I was caught off guard.

I expected him to shove his hardened length into my mouth so deep that he would put a dent in my throat, but instead I watched as he pulled up his shorts. He took my hand to make me stand up and join him as he sat on the edge of the bed.

"Jaxson, I love you. I have always loved you, but you and I both know that first night the name I called was not yours. We both know that I was his until I said my vows to you. Now, I don't know where he is in my heart, but I know you are in there. I don't want to keep you both, but I don't know how to let one of you go."

I stood up, unzipping the side of the dress and allowing it to fall. Then I pulled my bikini shorts off and stood in front of him. I took his hand and placed it over my heart.

"Right now, I need you to need me. I need you to want me so bad that you crave being near me. I want your mouth to water when you think of kissing me. I need you to be patient and understanding when I go all girlie on you and you don't get why I act a certain way. Most of all, I have to be the reason you get up every morning and face the day. Can you do this for me or are we over?"

Chapter 9

Jax stood up off the bed and placed his fingers around the back of my neck as his fingers stroked my cheeks. He pulled my face up and laid his velvety lips upon mine and kissed me sweetly.

I reached for his swim trunks again in hopes this is where this was headed. I didn't want to feel stupid again. As I fiddled with the strings, he made no move to stop me. Instead he deepened the kiss when I opened to allow his tongue entry.

His shorts fell as his flavor rushed me. Then he pulled my bottom lip in between his teeth and sucked it into his mouth. I moaned and he let my lip go and pulled back.

"Candice, you already have everything you requested from me, and more. I would give you the last beat of my heart if it meant you would live longer and carry me with you, but I will walk away if he is the one you choose. I will only fight for you as long as you want me to."

I wanted to cry at his words. Jax walked over to the tiny dresser and pulled out two black robes. He put one on himself and then came over and wrapped one around me. I watched as he pulled his phone out and sent a text. I made a mental note to check my messages now that we were away from Anti-Wi-Fi Island.

Jax took my hand and we headed out of the bedroom, down the corridor, and up to the deck. Jax took me to the nose of the ship where a hot tub sat. Then he turned a knob and the jets roared to life.

He walked over and untied my robe and let it hit the ground. Then I untied his and allowed it to fall. Jax stepped down into the hot tub and held out his hand for me.

I walked down the four steps into the steaming hot tub. I went to try and put my body fully into the water when Jax pushed me back until I was sitting on the top step.

He jerked my legs apart and I groaned with anticipation as I watched him lick his lips. Then, in one swift move, his tongue breached my folds as he held my waist up to his face, just barely above the water.

My head fell back on the edge of the tub as Jax devoured my clit. I grabbed onto the tiny ledge that outlined the tub as Jax's tongue licked and sucked until I was panting with need. I tried to wrap my legs around him and trap him, but he held me open. He was full of angry love and I was at his mercy.

Sweat broke out across my body as my toes curled and the pulsating nerves in my clit matched my heartbeat. My stomach tightened and my ample breasts grew heavy.

"You taste so sweet," Jax groaned and then he pulled me into the middle of the tub.

"Jax," I groaned with a need to come, but he had plans of his own.

Jax sat on the edge of a bench seat and placed me over his penis, facing away from him. I felt his fingers hold me open as I sank onto his hardened cock. When he was finally to the hilt, I felt the jets cross my clit. My toes curled and my mouth fell open.

"Let go, Candy," Jax growled as I shifted on him. The vibration of the water and the feel of him inside me had me on edge, but his voice in my ear launched me off like a rocket.

I jerked and wiggled as my screams echoed out into the ocean. I couldn't stop as I continued to make him stroke that rough patch inside me. Jax merely sat still and rode my climatic waves. It was when I came down that I knew he wasn't anywhere close to being done.

Jax bent my knee and turned me on him, which gave me a renewed need to have him. I faced my gorgeous husband and looked into his half-lidded eyes and saw the love and the pleasure that only I could give him.

"My beautiful wife," he whispered as I reached my hand up and took the Saint Michael's medal, that I had given him and held it tightly as I pulled Jax into me. I placed my lips on his and starting to slowly ride him as the jets flourished my back.

"Jax," I whispered when I finally pulled my lips away. He ran his hands up my back and placed a kiss on my neck. "I am so glad you picked me to be your wife."

Jax looked at me with a hint of confusion, but he didn't stray from his course. As I rode his hardened cock, his hands and lips were all over me.

I could feel him all over me. His hands left no skin untouched. His lips left a heated rush across my flesh. He was in the air I breathed and was the cause of my moans, and his hardened cock was taking me to places I had only written about in books.

"Tighten down on me," Jax growled and I did. Both of us groaned at the feel of each other. I didn't care who saw us. I was in a euphoric place where only the erotically hungry could go.

I lifted myself all the way up until the tip was barely inside and then I slammed back down on him. I ran my fingers through his hair as his lips took my pale pink nipple into his mouth. My back bowed and shifted him inside me. I was so close to another orgasm with him pulsating on that one rough patch behind my pelvis.

I whimpered as he licked my nipple and his arm around my waist held my hips still. I tried to wiggle to get that last inch to push me over, but he wouldn't let me move. I undulated and fought to get more or get away. My body was strumming, his penis was pulsating, and I was ready to plead to God to make him let me come.

"Candy," he murmured as one hand kneaded my ample breast, and his teeth grazed the other. I threw my head back with an impatient moan. I needed this orgasm like I needed him. "Say my name," Jax called out. He commonly did since I put that insecurity there, but I was really in no mood to talk. I wanted to bite his neck, so I did.

Jax pulled my hair into a pony tail and wrapped it around his hand. He gave a slight tug. I could have filled the hot tub with the liquid heat that flooded my thighs. He made me look right into his eyes as he pushed up into me harder and harder.

"Jax," I called out unintentionally. He was angry, but yet he still had a gentleness to him. "Jax, please," I begged as my breasts felt heavy and both of us were growing out of breath. He needed this as much as I did. I stared into his eyes as his body set the rhythm. I was strung tight like a guitar string and he only had to strum me once to make a beautiful orgasmic melody.

Jax let me go and I arched my body back and began a rapid back and forth motion, grazing my clit across his flesh as he planted kisses on my collar bone. I was supercharged and completely ready to make my song.

"I need you," I cried out, and Jax took me in his arms tightly. A frightening thought entered my mind and I shuddered. "Please Jax," I cried, not knowing what I needed. I started to panic, with thoughts of saying goodbye. As I wiggled and fought, Jax lifted me out of the hot tub and laid me on the cool deck.

He was over me, pushing my wet hair out of my face in an instant. I couldn't explain what was happening. I didn't even understand it.

"Candy, look at me," Jax demanded with a softened tone. I looked at him with tears in my eyes as my anxiety attack was finally coming down.

"Don't ever hate me," I cried. "I need you. I need this." I tried to explain, but as words failed to show their meaning, Jax understood. He slowly pushed in and out of me as he kissed away my tears. Tingles broke out across my body as his tender touch left fire behind.

"I can't hate you," he whispered and the rising moonlight took me to that euphoric place you read about in books, but only my husband had ever gotten me there.

"Jax," I screamed as his thumb brushed my clit. A galvanizing orgasm came out of nowhere, shocking me and sent electricity to every nerve ending. Jax stayed with me while I chanted his name over and over again. He groaned as my walls vibrated against him. It wasn't long before he pumped into me a few more times and found his own release.

His head fell over onto my shoulder and I wrapped my arms around him as we comforted each other under the stars in the night sky that shined down on us like diamonds.

It was just Jax and I, naked and alone, which was scarier than I had ever envisioned it. I had never been scared before, but right now, I was terrified of everything.

Chapter 10

I stood out on the white deck and stared into the sky above me that was covered in a thousand stars, listening to the waves crash softly against the ship. A cool breeze caressed my skin because the silk black robe didn't keep much out.

I held a glass of wine in my hand and asked myself what I was going to do about Chase. He was adamant about wanting me back, but even through my stale personality the last few days and knowing that I was wavering on our relationship, Jax stayed for me, and made me want to stay for him.

I tipped the glass and swallowed it all in a single gulp. As I swallowed down the ice chilled liquid, I looked into the ocean and wondered if the reason it was filled with water was because it stored the wishes of others.

Maybe my wishes were being held in an ocean of wishes because they weren't important enough to the heavens to be heard. You would think after having an insatiable time with my husband in the hot tub, and having everything I wanted, I would have no wishes. Sadly, I had wishes but none were for me and my faith was gone that they would ever be heard.

I leaned over and picked up the wine bottle and refilled my glass. The burgundy colored liquid was losing its chill so I guzzled it down. I hummed a little tune and closed my eyes to let the scenery take over my senses when I felt warm hands on my hips.

"There is my wife," Jax whispered as I leaned back and he sucked my ear lobe into his mouth. I lightly groaned and reached my arm up behind his neck to run my fingers through his brown hair. He turned me in his arms, as my cup slipped into the ocean. Jax quickly sat me up on the rail as he dropped his blue shorts down just enough to let his hard cock come out.

I bit my lip and grabbed the rails as he spread my legs and then he took me by the waist and sharply impaled his length into me. There was no hesitation, no foreplay. He didn't even untie my robe. Jax knew what he needed and with all the thoughts in my head, this was exactly what I needed.

"Fuck," I cried out as my body roared to life. I let go of the rail and threaded both my hands in his silky brown hair. As my flesh resisted, he pulled out and I bit down on his shoulder as he plunged in deep again.

My clit was throbbing as fire ran through my body. Jax bit down on my neck as my hips were pinned between him and the top rail. I was at his mercy with nowhere to go, and no reason to try to leave.

"Shit," Jax growled as I tightened down on him and locked my legs behind his back. I listened as he sucked air in through his teeth when he slammed into the hilt once more. I watched his eyes roll back in his head, when I leaned in and whispered that one word that I knew would drive him insane.

"Harder."

Jax pumped into me rigorously as my moisture continued to coat his dick. I wrapped my arms around his head when he lifted my legs up and hit the spot that left me a quivering mess.

"Jax," I called out as my head fell back and my moans were filling the night air. I squirmed to get away as the enormous orgasm was barely caged and raging to released. I curled my toes and leaned up to bite down on his arm.

"Oh, God!" I screamed, as pink lightning lit up the sky and my body thrummed to the flicker of lights. Jax seemed in sync with my weather once more because no matter where my eyes went, he was everywhere.

"Fuck, Candy," Jax growled as his hardened length stole my soul and left me breathless. I dug my nails into his flesh as the orgasm shot through my veins like the lights in the sky and steamrolled me, taking everything with it. I silently screamed as he continued his onslaught through the orgasm that never seemed to end. If I died today, I would go out completely satisfied with a smile on my face.

My head fell back once more as a raspy moan fell from my lips. I could feel Jax swelling inside me and knew he was close. I grabbed his face and forced him to look at me. Then I laid a hardened kiss on his lips and he growled as he found his own release.

As our breaths calmed, and Jax pulled out of me. He fixed his pants, and smirked when he saw his seed sliding down my thigh.

"What were you thinking about?" Jax asked a loaded question.

"You don't want to know," I replied and Jax crossed his arms.

"I want to know everything, Candice. I don't want any secrets between us."

"I was thinking about Chase," I whispered and closed my eyes. I kept thinking if I didn't see the hurt in his eyes then I couldn't have hurt him, but when I cracked an eye, Jax was no longer in front of me. He had walked into the cabin.

Thunder roared and rain began to cover me in dampness.

"Great fucking timing. You couldn't have opened up sixty seconds ago, before he asked me," I screamed to the clouds. I took a deep breath and closed my eyes. I knew I was messing up my life and my future, but I didn't know what the etiquette was. What do you do when the love of your youth returns from the dead? How do you get your heart back that beats for two instead of one? There were too many questions to answer, so I went below deck to take a shower and get some sleep.

Chapter 11

"Candy, wake up," Brooklyn's voice called out through my dream that was now a lost memory.

"Is the ship on fire?" I asked from beneath my comforter.

"No," Brooklyn laughed.

"Is there a hole and we are sinking?" I murmured.

"No, but you are getting up or else," Brooklyn retorted and I growled as I cocooned myself into the blankets.

Then in one swift move, I felt the comforter being ripped off the bed. Then all the sheets were drug off the bed and across the floor.

"Mark," Brooklyn yelled and I pulled the little bit of excess blanket over my head. "Pull her up to the deck."

I was ripped from my blankets and slung over a man as big as a grizzly bear's shoulder, and carried out while I protested to being awake before the sun was up.

"Best time to scuba dive is at sun up," Brooklyn assured me as I flipped her my middle finger.

"I warned you, she is not a morning person. Never has been," Jax yelled from the other side of the ship where he was getting oxygen tanks ready. "Get her some coffee and by the end of the first cup, she will be herself again."

The minutes ticked by like hours as I sat in a chair and watched everyone work around me. It wasn't long before they were handing me a suit and telling me to get dressed.

"Are there sharks?" I asked Brooklyn while my eyes were locked with Jax's. Then he pulled out his phone and sent a text. I had made a mental note to check my messages, but had forgotten it.

"It is the ocean," Brooklyn retorted and I handed the suit back to her.

"Come on, Candy Cane, you already gave it up, so they shouldn't be tracking you now," Jax laughed, but I went below deck and climbed in the bed.

Jax followed me below and sat on the bed as he set his phone on the stand. I rolled to look at him and wanted to cry. Hurting him hurt me, but I couldn't help the fact that Chase was front and center in most of my thoughts.

"If you want to stay here and get some sleep, then we will go out when we get back. I will take you to see a gorgeous waterfall that sits in a little cove," Jax finally caved and was going to let me and the sun sleep a little longer. "We will be back about lunch time." Jax stated and then leaned forward and placed a kiss on my lips.

"I love you," I called out as he started to leave. He turned and repeated it as I drifted off to sleep. I was being a party pooper, but I didn't know how to fix the exhaustion from trying not to feel anything for Chase.

I felt hot lips on my neck and rolled into the kiss. I moaned as those soft lips laid on mine. A hand reached inside my shirt and caressed my breast as the kiss was deepened and I groaned.

"Jax," I called out sleepily. Then the hands stopped and the kisses were gone. A chill fell over me and I cracked my eyes to see Chase in my room. "What the hell are you doing here? How did you get here?"

"You can't tell my touch from his?" Chase replied, ignoring my questions. Then I grabbed the blankets and pulled them up to my neck. My body was not responding to Chase's touch as it used to, but I didn't know if that meant I was over him or not.

"How did you get here?" I asked again. Tremors broke out across my body. I couldn't tell if I was just anxious or if we had breached that fine line into stalker behavior.

"I am a detective. I know how to follow someone," Chase sneered and stood, running his hand through his blond hair. "That was quite a show you put on last night. He didn't even bother to take off your clothes."

I cringed with each word he spoke, knowing that he had been watching. When he finally looked at me, I saw the agony in his eyes. The same pain I had been working so hard to avoid so no one felt it.

"You watched?" I asked as I pulled the blankets tighter. He was not acting like the man I remembered, but then I had changed over time too. Chase sat down and brushed his hand across my face.

"Candy, I wasn't going to say anything, but I wanted to make sure you were okay."

"Why?" I asked as confusion laced my words, and my heart rate refused to slow at the close proximity he was to me.

"I just don't want to see you get hurt," Chase uttered with hesitance.

"Why would I get hurt?" I demanded to know.

"Jax hasn't stopped seeing Vanessa," Chase spoke softly. I shook my head in denial and then Chase picked up Jax's phone to show me where she had called nine times just this morning. I took the phone and opened a text message that read 'I miss you. I love you!' Then there was a picture of the two of them as his wallpaper.

I had seen the picture before on his Facebook. She was pulling him by his Saint Michael's medal that I gave him and he was leaning in to kiss her pale face as her blond hair flowed down her back.

"Get the fuck out!" I screamed as I climbed out of bed. "Just leave!"

"Candy, please," Chase called out as I ran to the bathroom and began throwing up. He held my hair and placed a hand on my back to comfort me, but I felt ice cold. How could he make me fall in love with him if he wanted her?

"I need you to go, Chase," I spoke softly as tears filled my eyes.

"I'm sorry, Candy," Chase spoke softly and then walked toward the door.

"Chase," I rasped out and he turned to look into the bathroom with a softened look on his face. "How did you know he was still seeing her?"

"Let's leave it as I just knew. He is still my brother and partners never tell on each other. I should have never told you."

I started to sob and couldn't form words to roll off my tongue. There was no word vomit or angry bursts of nonsense anywhere to be found. My heart was shattered and I couldn't even breathe.

Chase got me up off the floor as everything that I was disintegrated and now Chase was picking up the pieces this time where Jax had last time. I felt feeble, and wanted to be more like Brooklyn or Kate. Those two seem to have it together.

"They don't," Chase whispered as I wiped my tears.

"What?"

"Brooklyn and Kate do not have it together. Brooklyn constantly looks over her shoulder because she deals with criminals all the time. Kate and the guy she is seeing, well I won't get into that because it's a long story, but your friends seem strong because their partners help carry the load, while you try to take it all."

I sat the phone on the bed that was open to their picture, and looked at how happy they both seemed. I had ruined that, because Chase had ruined me. Now Jax and Vanessa wanted to be together, but I was in the way.

"I didn't say anything," I replied because I had thought about Brooklyn and Kate, but never spoke it.

"You did, Candy. You have a tendency to when you are drunk or upset." Chase took my hand and I walked out to the deck. I looked out in the distance to barely see them playing in the water so far away.

I hesitated when I thought Jax's gaze met mine, but he was too far away to see me. Chase's hand hit the small of my back and chills ravaged me. I donned my favorite hoodie that belonged to Jax, but even it couldn't warm me. The sun glared down on the water, and blinded me from Jax at that moment.

"Can you take me back to the hotel?" I asked and Chase tilted his head. "I'm going to let him be happy. I am going to give him what he wants."

Chase squeezed my hand in support and pulled me into a hug. I looked over his shoulder to see Jax looking right at me. At least I thought he was.

"She can have him, since he wants her and not me," I murmured against his shoulder. My heart felt heavy and didn't want to leave, but I had seen the evidence in his phone.

Chase released me and then took my hand as we headed toward his boat. Climbing down the ladder on the side of the boat was simple, but leaving was hard. Chase took off so quickly, when I looked back, no one was in sight.

"Dad," I called out as I entered the baggage claim. I couldn't miss him in his jeans, wearing a red shirt that said 'Bride's Father' across the front. My dad waved his hand and gave me a sad smile.

"Hey Daddy," I whispered with tears in my eyes. I thought with taking a few extra days since they had to replace my passport that I would be able to get through a day without crying.

I was wrong.

"Is Chase with you?" My dad asked and I wanted to cry as my gut reminded me of what I had done to Jax with Chase's help. I would never be forgiven for leaving like that, while Jax would see what Chase did as betrayal. Those three little kids who took on the world and won had now fallen and died.

"I sent him home a few days ago," I whispered, trying to hold it together. My dad reached over and got my bag off the carousel then came back and took my hand.

"Candy Cane, you are skin and bones. Are you eating? Do you want to go to the Cafeteria for banana split waffles? My treat."

I merely shook my head and grabbed onto my dad as I began to cry on his shoulder. He dropped my bag, and wrapped his arms around me, into a full hug. For that one fleeting moment, I was that seven-year-old child whose mom had died and my dad enveloped me into his arms and held me until I fell asleep.

"I will hold you till the pain is gone, baby," he whispered, but it would never be gone. I just had to learn to live empty.

"You will never let me go then," I replied in a whisper.

"I will stay as long as you need me."

"I love you, daddy," I cried as he held me tightly. "Why wasn't I enough?"

"Baby, I think maybe you should talk to Jax. Running away wasn't the answer. I know you are hurting, but what you did was immature and reckless."

"Daddy, if he loves her and wants to be with her, then he should have just walked away. I get the need to take care of his partner's girl, but Chase came back for me. He doesn't have to pretend anymore," I sobbed into my dad's shirt as the words got harder to say.

"Honey, we all make mistakes. It is how we learn from them that makes the difference. I love you, but when things get hard, you react instead of thinking. I don't know what is going on with Jax or Vanessa, but you don't either because you ran."

"Oh, Daddy, this hurts so bad," I wept on his shoulder in an ugly cry I couldn't avoid.

"Candy," my dad called my name as I started to fall to the floor, grief and gravity taking control. "Candy, look at me." I tried to pull it together, but at the first touch of comfort, I broke like a fallen piece of glass. "Talk to him. What could it hurt to hear him out?"

"I'm dying without him now. I can't hear those words. I can't hear his voice say it is over," I cried and my dad sank to the floor and coddled me like a child until I was able to breathe again through the tears without the nausea. Voices echoed with murmurings, asking my dad if I was alright, and my mind flashed to Chase's funeral where I heard them all snicker in fake concern just like now.

I had to get it together.

"Where am I going to live?" I asked. I pulled back and my dad looked confused. "I sold the old house. Chase is living with you and Michelle, and I can't go to Jax's," I said with a shrug as I wiped snot on my sleeve, and stood up. I reached my hand down to my dad on shaky legs and saw security look at us.

It was time to go.

"I will kick Chase out if you want to come home. Michelle will understand." My dad smiled at me and took my bag in one hand and my hand in the other.

"Thank you for picking me up, but if I can't keep it together in an airport, maybe it is time I think about something more permanent. Like Virginia or back to California," I whispered.

"You are not running away because things are complicated and hard right now," my dad sternly spoke.

"I can fly anywhere for the book signings and can write from anywhere. I can call you every day and you won't have to coddle me when I cry," I rasped out as tears began to well up inside me again. "Besides, it is easier than the alternative."

"You mean it is easier than actually talking to your husband," Jax called out from behind us. I held my breath and looked to my dad. He had known Jax was right behind me and said nothing. I felt a mixture of mortification, fear, and relief in hearing his voice, but there was no way to avoid those words now. I closed my eyes and turned to face him. "It was so easy for you to just walk away. To not even talk to me. You didn't even leave a note. Always the martyr, right?"

"Jaxson," I whispered, as he walked up and took my bag from my dad. I don't think I have ever seen him more pissed than he was right now. I watched as he and my dad walked toward the escalator up to the exit, leaving me a ball of tears. I struggled to walk on shaky legs and a broken palate.

"You need to eat," my dad called out to me, and Jax agreed.

"I'm not hungry," I said.

"I don't care; you are eating," Jax replied and my dad nodded his head in agreement. This was going to be the longest meal ever.

Chapter 12

It seemed as though I had a welcoming party when Jax drove into the parking garage as I saw Brooklyn and Mark waiting in his black SUV. Kate and Eddie were also in a classic car like the ones my grandparents drove.

Kate was Brooklyn's very blond best friend. Not sure how they met, but those two could take on the world and win when they got along, but every now and then, Brooklyn's personality and Kate's mouth clashed and hell came to the surface so the devil himself could be in awe of the way those two fought.

Eddie used to be a suit and tie type person that they often spoke of, but since he became Kate's boyfriend he had taken on a new job as paramedic.

They really were the cutest couple. Her blond hair and blue eyes made her gorgeous, while she was a tad on the pale boney side, but Eddie didn't seem to mind as he was a linebacker in college and kept the physique. Kate stared into his brown eyes as she played with his hair and I was suddenly jealous that their relationship looked so easy.

I had wanted that.

My dad got out of his car and came around to open my door.

"Go and spend time with your friends. It will make you feel better, and then talk to your husband," my dad whispered as he placed a kiss on my cheek.

"Dad, don't go," I pleaded as Jax climbed out of his white F250.

"Candy, I have to go check on Chelle and Michelle. Give it an hour if you need me, call and I will come get you."

"Sir, with all due respect, she has proven she is a flight risk. I ask that you don't offer her a ride and allow us to handle her transportation needs today," Jax growled and I knew he was really pissed at me.

"Jaxson, I think that is what would be best right now." My dad smiled and shook Jax's hand. "Take care of my baby," my dad spoke softly. Jax agreed and then turned to look at me, while I wondered if he would really leave me. "Candy Cane, we all have to take responsibility for our actions. We all love you and care about you. We know you are struggling right now, but you left your husband at your wedding and again on your honeymoon. If your mother had done that, you wouldn't be here today. Think about what you are doing instead of reacting with immediate feelings. Your pain is not a one-way street, and you need to remember that."

Then my dad got into his waiting car, telling me they had planned this, and backed out of the parking garage. He didn't need to check on anything. This was his way of not allowing me to run away anymore. I was stuck at the mercy of others for transportation unless I started running to catch a cab, but there were three football playing men and two girls who ran miles for fun staring at me.

I wasn't going to get far.

Lunch was painful as I buried everything to sit quietly. I listened to Brooklyn tell Kate about their adventures on my honeymoon. Both girls lectured

Jax and I about how to make a marriage work, but I internally rolled my eyes.

Jax pulled my chair out and we began to walk out of the restaurant. Every bone in my body wanted to punch him when I saw the medal around his neck shine in the light. I wanted to make him taste his own blood for breaking my heart and tearing down everything I was, but he wasn't the only one to blame.

We walked along the sidewalk as we headed toward the parking garage to get the truck. Once we rounded the corner to go in the open bay, I jumped as Chase was standing in front of us.

I watched as Jax made a fist and his knuckles started turning white. Mark and Eddie closed in between them as Jax walked ahead of me.

"Jax," I whispered, but he didn't acknowledge me. It was as if I was invisibly silent.

Chase took a step toward him and crossed his arms. He was staking his claim as the alpha in this scenario, but he wasn't. My nerves started to sing an old familiar tune as I swallowed hard and moved toward what would surely be a bad situation. This could only end badly for me.

"Chase," Jax acknowledged him.

"Traitor," Chase replied, and I held my breath as I watched Mark and Eddie step out of the line of fire between the two. Brooklyn walked over to me. Kate walked to the side a moment later and started recording them for her own personal YouTube.

"I didn't do anything you didn't want me to do," Jax growled and Chase narrowed his eyes. "It is not like I stole your wife."

"You did Candy! I wanted you to make her happy. I didn't want you to put your dick in her," Chase responded and I took a step forward, but Brooklyn shook her head as she grabbed my arm.

"She was happy with my dick in her. Besides, you left her," Jax sneered.

"So did you. You left her all alone on her honeymoon for some guy like me to swoop in and be her knight in shining armor," Chase retorted.

"Guys," I yelled out, but I was still invisible while they had this you-took-my-toy confrontation.

"Knights are not full of themselves or asinine Neanderthals. You showed your true colors when you left."

"At least I came back for her," Chase growled.

"What bothers you more?" Jax started as he took another step and Chase cocked his eye brow. "The fact that she wants me, or the fact she doesn't want you?"

"Jax," I screamed, but no one cared what I had to say as Jax moved closer to Chase until they were nearly nose to nose.

"No, that is not it," Jax tsked and provoked Chase's irritation. "Tell me, does it bother you that it was my ring on her finger and my cock in her mouth or the fact that it was no longer yours?"

Chase threw a left punch and hit Jax square in the jaw. I screamed, but Brooklyn held me back with her Hulk Hogan death grip. I watched in slow motion as Jax's face showed fury and then it flat lined with zero emotion as he punched Chase in the stomach.

Chase bent over, grabbed his stomach, and coughed. I thought it would be the end, but then Chase charged Jax and they both flew into the street.

"Stop them," I shouted to Mark and Eddie, but they shook their heads and stood by to watch. "Please!"

"Candice, let them go," Mark bellowed as I started fighting Brooklyn to get loose. "They need to get this out of their system."

"No," I screamed as blood started pouring out of Chase's nose. Jax wasn't faring so well either as the shades of red and purple were already shadowing his body.

"You shouldn't have fucking left," Jax grit through his teeth as he put Chase in a lock with his legs. "You should have stayed if you wanted her."

Chase folded himself into a weird pyramid position to get loose and kicked Jax off of him before lunging over him.

"Please stop," I pleaded as tears filled my eyes. I couldn't watch, but I couldn't look away. These guys had been my whole life. My angel and my devil, and now they were a bloody pile of testosterone blocking traffic.

"You were not supposed to fall in love with her. She was mine and you crossed the line when you took her from me," Chase growled as he punched Jax in the face again. "Your job was to make sure she didn't get hurt."

"I didn't hurt her," Jax gruffly declared as he pushed Chase off him and got to his feet. He kicked him in the ribs as he looked over at me. Chase curled into a ball as he gasped for air. "You fucking hurt us both with your betrayal. You are the only traitor I see here. You are not my brother, my friend, or anyone of consequence. You are a liar and a thief."

Jax started to walk away with blood all over his shirt and his face swelling, but then Chase got up and charged him and they went sliding further into the street.

"Mark. Please," I shouted, because if someone didn't stop them, they were going to kill each other. He nodded his head and he and Eddie walked over and pried them apart.

"I'm fucking done, man," Jax called out when Mark let him go and he walked over to me. Brooklyn let me go to cry on his chest.

"You had a shot at a real life with me, but you left for that coward. Maybe we really don't have anything to talk about," Jax whispered as I leaned back to look at him.

"Bet's over," Chase called out as he climbed to his feet with his arm across the ribs. "Candy, did you know that when we started going after Andrew, Jax made a bet. We were standing outside a warehouse waiting on back up when our opportunity was fading fast. Then Jax put it out there."

"You don't know what you are talking about," Jax called out and I took a step away from him.

"We could have taken them and stopped everything. I wouldn't have had to go undercover, or knock up Christina. You wouldn't have been hurt, but this coward of a man didn't want to rush the room. He didn't want to save people," Chase growled as he took a few steps closer.

"Shut the fuck up!" Jax bellowed and everyone stayed still and waited to hear how I had been used in a bet, only I really didn't care.

"Jax was all concerned we would get shot and die. So, he bet me a night with you. If we waited for backup, and got in and out without anyone getting shot, I got to keep you whole and only mine," Chase continued as he stood toe to toe with Jax.

"What happened?" Kate whispered and broke the silence.

"Bad guy got away, Jax had a bullet graze his leg, and he got to stick his dick in Candy."

"You fucking shot me, but there was no bet!" Jax yelled and Chase spit in his face.

"I should have aimed at your head. Some brother you were. I stayed behind the door and watched them hurt those people while we waited for back up. *I waited to keep my girl*! I never thought you would follow through, but you took what wasn't yours and then you cheated on her. And you have the nerve to call me a coward. At least I told her."

"Fuck you! You don't know what you are talking about!"

"Tell me Jaxson, do you enjoy sloppy seconds and tasting the places where only my dick has been?" Chase growled.

Mark and Eddie rushed Jax who was ready to kill Chase, but no one was going to hold me back for that comment. I walked right up to Chase and kicked him in the balls. When he fell to the ground in a groan, I started kicking him in the ribs.

"Wear a fucking cup when you want to disrespect me!" I shouted as people started yelling my name. "Don't ever do this shit again. If you are dead, be dead!"

Then when I turned around, Jax was smirking at Chase. I had had enough. I walked over to Jax and slapped him with an open hand. When the shock covered his face, I leaned in.

"I love you, but I don't know if I even want to know you," I shouted,

"Candice-," Jax called out as Chase stood up and took a step toward me. "Candy-" Everyone was shouting my name, but I had exceeded the point of no return and needed to get away from everyone.

"Stay away from me!"

Chapter 13

"Candy, wait!" Jax yelled as I ran down the street. I heard his footsteps closing in behind me as I turned into an alley. The sky echoed to tell me a storm was nearby and building quickly.

Jax grabbed me and spun me around until I was facing him and my back was against the bricks of an old closed down pharmacy.

"You bet me. You used me to win some kind of game when I loved you," I screamed as I pounded my ineffectual fists on his chest. "You broke everything."

Then, in one swift move, his lips fell on mine as the sky opened up, drenching me in the rain I wanted to drown my sorrows in. He pushed his body against mine and I opened to him. Normally,

I tasted mint with his kiss, but in the rain, a new flavor of spearmint flooded me and I wanted to cry. He was strong and sweet, but he had shattered everything I was.

"I swear to you there was never any bet. His version of events is skewed. All I want is for you to want to be with me as much as I want to be with you," Jax whispered before his lips brushed over mine again. I pushed him away as lightning painted the sky above us. Soaked to the bone and out of breath, there was nothing to be said. Jax took my hand and walked me back to the parking garage. We climbed in his truck and sat in silence for what felt like hours, but was only a minute.

"Why her?"

Jax looked over at me and when I met his stormy grey eyes, I broke the hold I had on my emotions. It was as if the Hoover Dam had collapsed. I couldn't breathe, and dry heaves wracked my body.

I felt him lift me out of my seat and place me in his lap. I fell forward and cried on his shoulder.

"Candy, look at me," Jax whispered through my tears.

"I saw your phone," I rasped out.

Before Jax could reply, a loud bang sounded and immediately caused both of us to look to see a man wearing a leather jacket over a black shirt, holding a gun. Through my watering eyes, his belt buckle shined. As I wiped away my tears, I could make out that it had spikes on it. His gruff features made him look like Satan himself.

"Get down," Jax shouted and I dropped across his body as he turned the truck on. A shot rang out and his window splintered. My tears evaporated from the fear and anxiety that was coursing through my veins. Jax shifted into drive leaving the tires playing catch up as they squealed.

I peeked up just enough to see Jax aim the nose of his truck at the man and hit the gas. I felt his hand come down over my head and he murmured 'you're safe' over and over again, and the truth was I felt like he would save the day.

I slid over to the passenger's seat to get the gun from the glove box as quickly as I could, but I raised up and froze when I saw the man jump out of the way. It all happened in slow motion before my eyes. A new shot rang out and pierced the window and into Jax before it ever made a sound in my ears. Jax sped past him, hitting the arm that told people when to enter the garage. Four more shots rang out and the back window shattered.

"Fuck," Jax called out as he sped away from the garage. After a few minutes of everything continuing in slow motion, I looked over to confirm my worst fears. I swallowed hard as Jax had blood dripping down his shirt.

"Oh my god," I called out and shifted my legs off him so he could drive and I could apply pressure. "You got shot," I pointed out the obvious as if I had just entered this reality.

"It is probably just a graze," he spoke calmly. "Are you okay?"

"I'm fine," I replied as I felt my body for cuts and bullet holes. "Was that a friend of yours?" I asked sarcastically.

"To be honest, I have never seen him, but I will find him, and we will see if he likes being shot at."

"Where are we going?" I asked quietly.

"Our house. I need to get cleaned up, call this in, and leave you somewhere safe."

I reached over and grabbed my purse with my phone in it. I sent a text to Kate to have Eddie meet us at the house.

"Jax, maybe you should take me to my dad's," I whispered. "I will be safe there."

"No, we need to talk and I am not leaving you with Chase," Jax growled as he picked up his phone and hit the speed dial.

I listened as he conveyed the event that just happened to Mark and report the description of the man. I swallowed hard as Andrew came to mind and all we had been through. Would life always consist of someone shooting at the men I loved?

We arrived at the house to see the NYPD there, waiting to take our statements. Eddie latched on to the sight of blood and immediately went to work on Jax. I watched as they peeled the shirt off Jax to see it was not a scratch. The bullet went clear through his shoulder under the collar bone.

My issues suddenly seemed transparent as the flashing lights on the cars hypnotized me. I could care less of what the world thought. I didn't care if I was the other woman, because he was worth fighting for. I didn't care what my head said. Chase had become a forgotten memory and Jax became my future.

"Mrs. Monroe, did the assailant say anything?" Detective Costello asked as I stared at my husband and all the blood that trickled down his hardened chest.

Everything in my world changed in that moment. I had left him on our wedding day. I left him on our honeymoon, but yet he was at the airport waiting for me. I acted like a complete ass, but he wanted to at least talk about it before we drew up papers and ended what we worked so hard to build.

"Mrs. Monroe, are you okay?" Detective Costello asked again, but I was in another world. I heard him call for a medic, and Jax's eyes met mine. Eddie was doing something to the wound and Jax flinched.

Everything else went into a haze as I walked toward him. I walked past the voices yelling that they had to take my statement. I ignored pleadings from Eddie's partner to allow him to check me over.

As I came upon my husband, I saw him flinch again. I took in the needle that Eddie was using. I knew if Eddie was stitching him up here instead of going to the hospital, it meant my husband was getting ready to hunt down the man responsible.

I walked right in between his legs and I placed my hand behind his neck.

"I will be his pain killer," I whispered as I grabbed the bottom of Jax's hair and pulled his lips to mine. I felt an instant electricity as our lips locked.

I licked his lips and he opened to allow my tongue to slide inside. I may have started the kiss, but his flavor overwhelmed me and suddenly it was his hand in my hair holding me in place so we didn't move while he was being stitched.

He moved his lips to my cheek and down to my neck as his hand held my hair and moved me wherever he wanted me. I let go of his hair and held on to his waist as involuntary moans left my lips when he ran his tongue from my shoulder to the base of my ear.

I was breathing fast as he bit down on my shoulder and then he left a kiss in its place. Forgotten were the people around us and the events that took place. The only thing in our intimate bubble was Jax and I. His lips were taking me to that euphoric place where only he could get me.

My clit throbbed as I linked my fingers in the belt loop of his jeans and he sucked my earlobe into his mouth. My body was on fire, and wanted to explode as my knees grew weak. Jax pulled my hair again and made me face him. He pressed his lips to mine, pushing his tongue inside. I nearly melted as bliss invaded my core.

Jax pulled back to let me catch my breath as the sound of clapping in the background caught my attention. He let go of my hair, and I looked over at Eddie.

"Is it done?" I asked breathlessly.

"I was done ten minutes ago," Eddie stated as he started to laugh.

"Woo-hoo, free admission to porno day," Kate called out and I turned to see everyone had been watching. My cheeks turned crimson, and I wanted to hide behind my husband as the guys sounded out catcalls. "Get it girl!" Someone shouted and I turned and placed my head down on Jax's shoulder.

"Don't be embarrassed," Jax stated as he lifted my head up to face him. "Those were the best stitches I have ever gotten," he stated with a chuckle.

I finally went back and gave my statement to the waiting detectives who couldn't stop smiling at me.

"What?" I asked everyone as they continued to smile at me. "Distraction is everything when it comes to pain," I tried to explain, but it was pointless. We were newlyweds and the NYPD was having a blast picking on our display of affection, no matter why it happened.

"I heard I should have brought popcorn," Brooklyn chuckled as she walked up to me. She and Mark had been at the scene and were playing catch up now that they were here with us.

"I could have made a small fortune on movie tickets," I replied with a laugh. "Did you find him?" I asked as my demeanor changed to serious, and we walked away from Jax.

"How long was it between the shots and when you called it in?" Mark asked as he walked up behind Brooklyn.

"Not long, maybe two or three minutes," I replied and worry crossed their faces. "What's wrong?" I asked and tried to prepare myself for any answer they gave, but you cannot be ready to hear that someone wanted to kill your husband.

"The shell casings and security footage were gone. This is looking like a professional hit," Mark stated and my body jerked as shock took over.

"Wouldn't he have got him with the first shot?" I asked. I wasn't a police officer, but I was an author, and the story wouldn't make sense to miss.

"If he is a pro, then he missed on purpose, meaning it is a warning. Someone has a bullseye on Jax," Mark replied and I grabbed my stomach as nausea swirled. "Candice, do not worry. I would take a bullet for him," Mark responded ignoring the perturbed look crossed Brooklyn's face.

"Is my husband going to die?" I asked and no one said anything. I turned and looked over at Jax as I tried to keep the sobbing under control. I had been through the emotional ringer and it was looking like it would never end.

"Where was Chase when this happened?" I turned back and asked as Brooklyn and Mark looked at each other. "You were there; did he drive off? Was he still inside?"

"There was a blood pool at the garage, but no body. We haven't identified whose blood it is yet, and Chase has not been located," Brooklyn replied, sounding professional.

"You mean, I just got him back and he could be dead?"

"We don't know anything yet, but I am placing two officers in unmarked cars in front of your house. Jax won't be happy about it, but tonight you both can rest easy," Mark spoke up and placed a hand on my shoulder as if to comfort me.

"You both need to be on lockdown to force you both to talk about what happened in Saint Lucia," Brooklyn muttered. "He had the whole damn island looking for you, and the coast guard came out to search for your body. The man was going insane until your dad called the resort."

"I'm sorry you went through that," I whispered as I heard thunder echo through the air. My eyes misted as guilt invaded my core.

"Look, we love a good mystery, but not when it involves those we love. We don't want your apology. We want you to never do that shit again," Brooklyn's words were laced with a hint of anger, but then she took a deep breath and wrapped her arm around Mark's waist as he pulled her into his side. "We love you both and this lockdown is a perfect opportunity for you to apologize to him for that, and talk about whatever the hell is going on. What the hell *is* going on? Why did you bail?"

"Chase came to the ship. He said that Jax was still seeing Vanessa. I didn't want to believe him, but the evidence was in his phone," I spoke softly it was almost a silent whisper as the words left my mouth. I felt as though if I gave it more volume it made it real.

"Candice, I cannot see him doing that. He loves you," Brooklyn spoke up and then took my hand in hers.

"No way. Jax is my partner and I would know. There was never anything between them that wasn't for show. I have never seen Jax care about anyone like he does you, and the man wouldn't have time because he is always chasing you," Mark chastised, making me feel two inches tall.

"Candy," Jax called out behind me. I turned to look at him with rain droplets cascading down my face, hiding my tears as the sky opened up. "They want us inside the house."

Jax held out his hand for me and I took it. He pulled me to his side.

"Would you both like to come to dinner next weekend?" Jax asked, as something crossed his face and Mark immediately accepted. I was lost in the hidden messages that were happening before me.

It seemed someone had snapped their fingers and everything fell into place. The excess police cars were rolling away. Security was in place to keep us safe, and my heart was on the line as there were no more distractions. There were no more bullets. There was nothing to keep him from explaining about Vanessa, and there was no way to hide from my immature actions of leaving him on our honeymoon.

Why couldn't I bet my way out of this?

Why couldn't the shooter open fire on me right now? Getting shot sounded so much more appealing than hearing my husband talk about his girlfriend, but it was about to happen.

Chapter 14

I watched as my husband set our coffee cups on the black countertop in the kitchen and pulled out a bag of Tim Horton's coffee. He was brewing a pot because he knew I was addicted to the caffeinated flavors of their coffee. It told me he thought this was going to be a long talk.

I went and sat on the grey couch and stared at the wedding gifts that were stacked beside the fireplace against the blue wall. The sixty or so boxes that we had yet to unwrap taunted me because their contents were supposed to be gifts for finding a happily ever after and it seemed I was still waiting for mine.

As the coffee percolated, I looked anywhere but in the direction of Jax. I looked out the window to see the remnants of rain. I looked at my desk where I spent countless hours. I took in my new typewriter that was on a stand beside my work space. I got up and walked over to it. I slid my finger across the keys and closed my eyes.

I could still hear my mom's voice explaining subject verb agreements and placements of my fingers on the keys. I could almost smell the gingerbread that she would make for when I was able to compel a great adventure in a story. I could hear her laughter when I would press on the keys harder, thinking it would force a story to come.

"Candy," Jax's voice carried me out of memory lane and I turned to see him holding my coffee cup in his hand. I half-smiled as I walked over and took it from him.

"Do you think our parents, who are in heaven, are happy about us getting married so quick?" I asked as I walked over to the couch and set my coffee cup down on the small black coffee table. It had replaced the glass one that somehow broke during the fight between Christina and I.

"I think they are happy we are together; timeline wouldn't factor in. My parents adored you, they always said that you were the daughter they never got to have," Jax replied and then took a drink of his coffee.

"I remember your mom taking me to the cemetery to visit my mom. This one time, we were standing there and I was crying. I couldn't stop the waterfall down my face. I didn't want to put my flowers down on her grave because then I would have to say goodbye to my mom again. Your mom walked up and laid down beside my mom's grave. She patted the ground and told me to lay down too.

"We lay there talking about everything until the sun had fallen and the stars had come out. Your mom looked at me and asked if I wanted to stay the night with my mom. I nodded and there we stayed. I woke up as the sun was rising, and your mom was smiling at me.

"Then, as we got ready to go home, I placed my flowers down and your mom said 'your mom is no longer alone under the stars because you left a piece of your dreams behind for her.' I didn't understand it then, but when she died, I once again slept out under the stars so your mom wouldn't be alone either."

"I remember. You had us all out there sleeping in the cemetery," Jax gave me a half-smile and sipped his coffee. The silence was deafening in the house. We needed to talk, and I knew Jax was waiting on me to start, but I didn't want to hear him tell me why Vanessa was in his phone. As long as the words were not said, I could pretend that it wasn't real.

"Are we going to talk or reminisce?" Jax asked and I knew I was running out of time. I grabbed my coffee and held it tight. I shut my eyes tight and prepped myself for the Earth-shattering blow that was coming.

"I'm ready," I whispered.

"For what? A colonoscopy? Why the hell are you holding your eyes shut and sitting like you are about to take a hit?" Jax demanded to know.

"If I focus, it won't hurt so bad," I sighed and opened my eyes. "I know that sounds stupid, but I know what is coming, and am desperate to never feel the pain I felt on the ship. I am living in this place called denial where it is not real until you tell me about her."

Jax got up and walked over to the kitchen where his phone was sitting on the counter. Then he walked over and handed it to me.

"There is no one else," Jax stated. "Look for yourself if you don't trust me."

"That is a double edged sword. If I open your phone to show you, then you think I don't trust you, but if I don't, I have no proof."

Jax merely waved his hand to tell me to get on with it. I opened his phone and the wallpaper was still that photo of Vanessa. I turned the phone and showed it to him, but he didn't say anything. Then I opened his messages and pulled up the text.

"What is this?" I asked as I showed it to him.

"Press call," he stated confidently. I pressed it and let it play on speaker. With each ring, I was thinking of all the horrid things I could do to her, but then the voicemail came on and I was blasted with a voice from the past.

"Hey you know who this is and you know why you called, so leave a message and fill me in." A raspy version of Chase's voice echoed through the house.

I was mortified and began to cry. Jax took the phone from my hand and scrolled to the letter V in his phone. He pressed call. After two rings, she answered.

"Hey stranger, how goes the married life?" She asked sweetly.

"Well, it seems someone wants Candy to think you and I are still seeing each other," Jax responded.

"Not sure if it will help, but I can talk to her if you want me to," she replied.

"Thanks, V. I will offer it up to her if she needs to hear it from you. Hey, if you ever need anything, you have my number," Jax spoke softly as my hands covered my face.

"Thanks, it is always good to have a detective for a friend. Maybe you can help me with my parking tickets," she laughed, and they ended the call.

Jax stood up and walked to the kitchen while I quietly sobbed.

"I'm sorry," I finally spoke up as Jax topped off his coffee.

"Are you sorry for running off at our wedding? Are you apologizing for telling me you loved another man? Are you trying to make amends for escaping our honeymoon and leaving me to think you had been kidnapped or killed? Is this supposed to cover up the fact you didn't trust me? Tell me *exactly* what you are sorry for," Jax bit out each sentence. The more he spoke, the angrier he seemed to get.

"All of it," I whispered quietly. Then I stood up and walked into the kitchen. "I know that my flight or fight response leans over to *run-bitch-run*, and loving me comes with that risk. I know it is a lot to ask, but I have to hope that you love me enough to overlook it."

"You want me to ignore the fact that you keep running off?" Jax stated sarcastically. "I am supposed to just forgive and forget that you run from my touch, my love, and all of me."

"I'm sorry," I said, a little louder this time.

"Are you sorry now because I got shot and it scared you? Or are you actually really and truly sorry?"

I took a deep breath. I had seen him angry a thousand times, but he was so rarely angry at me that I didn't know how to soothe him. I didn't know what to say to grant him comfort that I wouldn't run away again.

Would I run again?

"Jax, when Chase showed up, every fear I ever had rose to the surface and clashed with the guilt for moving on with my life. I came to the conclusion that I wasn't good enough, pretty enough, or sexually educated enough to keep you. But I am a selfish person, and not so long ago, I leaned on you at a funeral and asked you to never leave my side. I know I haven't been a good wife, and I know I don't deserve you, but I am asking you now. Please don't walk away."

"Candice, I have never left you. I have always been where you needed me to be. You are the one who keeps running. You are constantly leaving me. Do you want to be married to me, or did you say yes because you didn't want to feel lost anymore?"

I walked over to Jax and wrapped my arms around his muscular tanned body and whispered against him.

"It has always been you that I wanted. It just took me a long time to see I was on the wrong path with the wrong man. I know I screwed up, but I am asking you for another chance."

"I don't want to leave, but how many more chances do you expect me to give?" Jax asked as he turned to face me. I laid my head on his chest with my arms still wrapped around him and wondered the same thing myself.

"Just stay by my side," I whispered. "I don't deserve understanding or forgiveness, but I have to ask you to grant it because I can't live without you." I started to cry as I slid off his lap, dropping to my knees as I pleaded for my heart.

"Please Jax, I can't promise you I won't screw up, or burn your dinner. I won't promise to fold the laundry or not ignore you when reading a book. What I can swear to you is that every morning, I will be a pain in the ass to wake up. I will kiss you goodnight every night. I can promise I will worry every time you go to work and that I will occasionally bring you lunch that I buy from somewhere else and pretend I made it.

"I will try my best to stop running. I promise to be territorial and jealous, and I swear I will do my best to keep killers in the books and away from us. I will give you everything I have to give because you and I are two pieces of a full puzzle. No one else fits us, and we aren't whole without each other's interlocking piece. I will give you anything you want, just please don't say it's over."

"I know what you want me to say, but the truth is, you didn't trust me. You didn't let me be your partner, so I can't say anything. You can't even promise that you won't run, you just said you would try. I can't give you an answer because I need time," Jax replied and stepped around me to go upstairs as I lay on the floor to cry.

Chapter 15

Life is never what you thought it would be. As a child, they say you can be anything you want to be and I suppose you can if you sacrifice everything about yourself to get it. When my father used to warn me about how complicated life would get as I aged, I always knew I could get through it with Chase and Jax by my side.

Only I didn't have either now.

I sipped the coffee I had made as I sat in a chair on the back deck. Jax had went upstairs hours ago and left me to drown in my own emotions. I completely deserved it, and wanted to leave to give him space, but the officers out front made me stay on the property.

The stars twinkled in and out of the storm clouds as they quickly rolled over us. Rain came in bursts tonight, making my entire body want to go to the wishing well that sat in the middle of the yard. I wanted to make a wish, but my head told me it was pointless. There is no one granting wishes on the water or the stars. There is no such thing as luck or magic. Life is what it is.

I had spent the entire night out here staring at that gray brick well. I wanted to destroy it like I had my marriage. I stood up and walked off the deck when a flicker caught my eye. I turned to see the cellar doors had light shining from them.

Jax had bought this house because it has a wine cellar that ran under the house, but we never went in there. I took a sip of my coffee and sat it on the railing. I then walked over and lifted the wooden doors that were lined with metal embellishments.

Once the door was open, I could see a flicker of light so I grabbed my coffee and walked down the twelve steps into the red brick cellar. The wine cases were gone, and bookshelves lined the walls. The room smelled of sawdust and books. The soft lighting came from the sconces that flickered with flame bulbs and lined the brick walls.

I walked up to the first book case and studied the books. They were all second and third editions of really old books. Thomas Hardy, Charles Dickens, Henry James, and Charlotte Brontë, along with the rest of the classics, lined the walls.

I ran my fingers across them as I sipped my coffee. I walked from shelf to shelf as thousands of books beckoned me to read them, to hold them, to love them.

At the back of the room, where the air purifier used to sit, was a set of cream colored chaises, and a small black lamp that read 'Read More Books' across the front, sitting on a glass stand of books. There was a small desk on the opposing wall with a laptop that had a pink bow on it.

I walked over and opened the card that sat under the bow and opened it.

You gave me the best gift of all when you said I do. Since nothing I do can compare with what you have given me I wanted to give you the one thing you wanted the most and never got. Your own library.

I dropped my cup down on the hardwood floor as I held the note to my chest. Coffee spilled all over the hardwood as the cup shattered. He loved me and I had thrown it all away. I knew why Chase lied like he did, and sadly I couldn't be angry because I would go the distance if I had to for either one of them, but it was costing me my marriage.

I slid down the brick wall as I held that letter in my arms and cried. I could feel myself losing him. I felt what we had built sliding through my grasp, but as the thunder returned, I had to admit that if we were meant to be, we would be and if not, then I would have to wish him well on his way.

I stood up and closed the cellar doors as the rain began to pour inside. I heard the air turn on and the moisture from the rain was slowly fading from the room. He had factored in everything except whether or not I would stay. When I turned around, one of the book shelves had a glow around it by my desk.

I wiped my last tear and walked toward it as the storm raged above me. I pulled it to see it was a door. I stepped inside an old chimney that had been taken out and all that remained was the brick outline and a ladder.

I put the note in my mouth and climbed up the extra-large chute, my curiosity piqued, and anything was better than crying. There was a small platform that I stepped onto as I reached the top. I climbed off and noticed the door in the red clay bricks. I pulled the handle and the door slid to the right on tracks.

I took a step in and was in a dark room. Something soft hit my arm as I took the note from my mouth. I stuck my arms out and pushed the heavy cloth to see light under the edge of another door. I took a deep breath and felt for the doorknob. I found it and as quietly as I could, I turned it and cracked it open.

I was in Jax's guest room closet. Now I knew how Chase had gotten up here and no one saw him. Then my heart dropped as I wondered if he was in here that night that Jax and I were first intimate. I tip-toed out into the room as I heard the shower running. I started to go back downstairs until I heard my husband's beautiful voice. He was singing "So Far Away" by Avenged Sevenfold. It was funny how that song carried a different meaning every time I heard it.

The first time I heard it, I felt comfort from Chase being gone from us, and it led me into Jax's arms that night. And now I hear it and I feel loss, like my husband is already gone. The song was giving me chills.

The song spoke the truth. I didn't know how to live without him, but it seemed I was already gone. Jax's voice made me weepy and while I didn't want to impose on his space, I couldn't walk away. As long as his voice carried the song, I was pinned in place. I closed my eyes and envisioned him dancing with me to the lyrics he was singing.

"What are you doing in here?" Jax asked as I opened my eyes to see him putting away his gun as he stood wrapped in a towel.

"Dreading dawn," I replied and Jax tilted his head. All the begging I had done was pointless because we both needed to know where my heart was. "Even though I will always love you, we both know that when the lockdown is lifted, I am gone."

"I won't chase you, Candy," Jax whispered as he put on his shirt. I watched my husband get dressed and everything in me wanted to run to him and have every bit of him, but as he put on his shorts, I knew exactly what I had to do. It all became clear.

"I don't want you to." I nearly choked on my words, but it had to be said. "You came for me in California, but walked away. Then I came back because of work, and you came for me outside the bar. You came for me when I ran off to the lighthouse to tell me you loved me. You chased me when I ran out of our wedding, and you looked for me when I left on our honeymoon. I will always wonder why the Earth stops spinning when you're gone, but I will never know unless you let me be free. Stop bringing me home. Wait and see if I come back on my own. Let me sort my head out."

"If you don't come back?" Jax asked and I watched him try to hide the redness invading those gorgeous grey eyes. I looked away to see the moonlight dancing across the floor, telling me my storm was gone and so was my marriage.

"If I don't, then we were never meant to be," I hoarsely rasped through the unshed tears I was holding back. I tried to hand him the card from the library but Jax pulled me up against his chest.

"I won't wait for you, Candy. I can't. Every time I have to chase you I am waiting to see if you run again," Jax stated as he hugged me tightly.

"I know," I whispered and it was done. There was nothing left to be said. I once again would be packing my luggage in the guest room where our adventure started. I would once again walk away from the only man I loved fully.

I picked up my suitcase, as Jax sat on the bed, and watched me pack. When the silence gutted me, I broke the quiet. "How long are we going to pretend that today didn't happen and you don't have a bullet wound?"

"I'm not pretending. I got shot. It is not a big deal," Jax stated casually as he did the macho thing and hid his emotions.

"*No-big-deal?*" I enunciated each word.

"He missed everything vital," Jax stated and then took off his white shirt as if to show me it was just a scratch, but it wasn't.

"He missed everything except your body!" I exclaimed as a freak out was coming and there was nothing I could do to hold it back.

"Candy, I'm fine," he stated as he pulled me into him and I breathed along with him to avoid exploding on him. "It isn't your problem anymore," Jax murmured as I pulled away. I had to count to a hundred before I could speak again.

"Jax," I whispered. "If someone is trying to kill you, what do we do?"

"You won't do anything. You will go live your life like you want and I will get them before they get me," he replied with confidence. The same confidence I heard before Chase got shot and flashbacks echoed in my mind as my body quivered.

"I have to ask this," I started and he looked like he was done talking. "Do you have your things in order? Paperwork? Should we talk about how you want your service? I am still legally your wife. I want to know that your wishes are carried out."

Jax walked downstairs and over to my desk. He pulled open the bottom drawer that doubled as a filing cabinet. He pulled out a folder labeled 'death' and handed it to me.

I opened it and saw a will, and a power of attorney for medical decisions. Then, in the back, there were two envelopes. One was addressed to me, and the other was addressed to 'the one who loves her last.' I fell to the floor as this all became real.

"This is why you can't keep bringing me back. I need to be gone because you can't leave me – you can't leave like he did," I wept.

Chapter 16

A few weeks later, I had eaten too much as we sat around the dinner table conversing about nothing while we drank wine. It was weird being back in Jax's house, but I was grateful I was invited until I saw Vanessa was there. I stayed at my dad's since no one had seen Chase in the three weeks since the shooting.

In the darkest recesses of my thoughts, I had to wonder if he came back only to die again. I questioned if the timing was all coincidental because they shot at Jax too. Was this one of their cases?

Vanessa sat next to my husband as Mark and Brooklyn sat on either side of me across from him. Kate and Eddie sat at the ends of the table. I tried to sit by Jax, but *Skanknessa* had other plans and the second I went to get a bottle of wine, she took my seat.

I knew we were separated. Hell, we barely spoke at dinner, but it irked me that she was here and shoving her floatation devices that her bra had pushed up to her chin in his face at every turn. I knew she had been innocent in everything that went down and she had been the one that was hurt, but it didn't change my feelings of wanting to force her at gun point to walk across a floor full of Legos while on fire.

"Let me clean up and I will bring out dessert," Vanessa called out and Jax protested, but she placed a hand on his shoulder to reassure him it was fine and he flinched.

I grabbed the steak knife on the table and placed it in my lap. Brooklyn shook her head at me, and I glared. Kate silently clapped her hands quickly as she was ready for the WWE match to begin.

"Oh, I'm sorry, I didn't know you were hurt," she stated with a wink, her low cut dress flashing cleavage once more as she reached over to get his plate.

"Too many witnesses," Brooklyn whispered and Mark's hand fell over mine as my grip tightened on the knife.

"What is a better alibi than the NYPD, Assistant District Attorney, and a paramedic?" I whispered back to Brooklyn.

"Let's do this," Kate snickered under her breath as she pretended to cough. "Fuck her up," she coughed again.

"Must be something in the air with the weather changing," Kate spoke out loud and took a sip of water as Eddie looked concerned about her coughing. She sent me a wink.

"Must have been a hell of a work week if you are sore. I used to be a masseuse. I can work that out if you want me too," Vanessa stated, while I silently repeated, *'I will not stab her. I will not stab her. I will not stab her. Okay, I might stab her.'*

"Here, let me give it a try," she started and I stood up. All eyes were on the knife that was sitting by my thigh. I had white knuckled it and Mark's hand had yet to leave mine.

"Let me rub him and you can bring out the dessert," I politely stated as Jax tilted his head, trying to read me. Vanessa flashed a cheerful grin and took the dirty dishes to the sink. Jax gave me a questioning look and I merely tightened the grip on my knife.

"We are just friends," he whispered before she came back with a tiramisu she had made for *my husband* as she knew it was his favorite. Anything with coffee or expresso was our thing and she was impeding on it.

"Good, she needs friends to be her pall bearers," I whispered back and gritted my teeth. I didn't even factor that his statement of we were just friends was meant about me and not Vanessa, but his face was screaming it at me.

"You are too cute when you try to be bad ass, but let me show you how it is done," Kate stated as Vanessa came back and set the dessert down. Kate stood up and kinked her glass.

"I want to make a toast," she started with a wink for me. "I want to congratulate Candice and Jax for making the vow to love and cherish each other above all others. We know there are rocky roads ahead, but we saw this bond coming, and are so glad you got past every whore, and killer, that interfered on your journey. May you all find the happiness that was designed by the stars, and created just for the two of you. May you live in merriment where sluts don't have to be cut, and killers die from a papercut." Then she turned and looked at Vanessa, whispering, "No offense," and continued. "To Candice and Jax. The best friends we will ever know. May you find the road that works for you both," then she took a drink.

I lifted my drink and took a sip as vexation crossed Jax's face. Brooklyn was trying to stifle a laugh as Mark kept his hand on mine, and Eddie seemed oblivious as to what she was talking about.

"Excuse me," Vanessa stated as she stood up and went out the back door. Jax got up and went after her.

"Don't ever give a toast at my wedding," Brooklyn laughed. "I can only imagine what you would say."

"Too much," Kate asked and I shook my head. "What is she doing here?"

"I don't know. This is the first time I have spoken to him since we separated, but she needs to find someone else to hang out with."

"Honey, you made the choice to leave your husband and now he can't have a friend or girlfriend?" Brooklyn replied professionally. "You cannot have it both ways. Either he is yours and we can cut her, or he is not and you have to back off."

I put the knife on the table, got up, and walked to the back door. Guilt was fettering my decision making. I opened the door to see Vanessa was facing me and Jax had his back to me. They were standing in the backyard next to the wishing well Jax had built for me to match the one he had built at the park. She ran her finger over the grey bricks while my mind flashed visions of implanting one in her skull.

I had to shake my head to get rid of the violent thoughts as I walked over to the well.

"I'm sorry for what was said. Kate was merely trying to make me feel better because Jax and I just separated and you are here touching him," I stated sarcastically.

"I touch everyone," Vanessa replied. "I'm friendly and I was a masseuse. I was just trying to help."

"Bless your heart," I replied as Kate laughed from the back door. "Jax is hurt because he was shot, and that is nothing you can fix," I responded and she looked at Jax with concern. I wanted to make her fertilizer and plant a rose garden over her, but I was going to be the bigger person.

"I apologize if I crossed any lines, but Jax and I are friends. You are going to have to get used to it. Taking pot shots in toasts won't make me go away."

My mouth twitched and focused on her words that I would have to 'get used to it.'

"I think I am going to call it a night, and leave."

"Actually Candice, I invited you over to give you something," Jax replied and walked inside the house. Then he came back out with a manila folder with an attorney's name across the front.

"What is this?" I asked, even though I already knew.

"Your freedom," Jax replied, and I wanted to die. I had to hold it together long enough to get away from the house.

Chapter 17

"Ready to go house shopping?" Brooklyn stood in my doorway with her blond haired blue eyed friend, Kate, who made me sick with how much food she could ingest and not gain a pound, and always had Skittles in her purse.

"Sure, I just put on my jeans and Jax's Metallica hoodie. Five minutes earlier and you would have seen me in nothing but a towel. So, give me a minute." Then, when I picked up my purse and the envelope of money my dad had given me, I continued, "Are we really house shopping for Kate or did my dad send you on this mission?"

"Candy, you know I just love your eye for detail. So, you are going to go pick the perfect place for you so I can have it but you never know. You might find what you are looking for out there," Kate stated as she wrapped an arm around me.

I hadn't seen Jax in a month. I never signed his papers, but I never called him either to beg him to come back. Thinking of him as my happily ever after scared the hell out of me, especially when people were out to get him. I occasionally finagled information out of Brooklyn about him, but she was pretty tight lipped. I had found out someone took the lug nuts off his truck tires and cut his brake lines. If he hadn't been going as slow as he was, he would have died.

"Chase is meeting us for lunch. I hope that is okay," I spoke softly. He finally showed up when they put out an APB for him because the blood in the garage was a match to his blood type, but they were still awaiting DNA.

The Chief immediately pulled him in and had him working on finding out who shot Jax. Chase seemed to pop up like a pimple on prom night. Always in the wrong place at the wrong time, and you don't know how the hell he got there.

"He can come, and I won't castrate him if he picks up the bill," Kate said and I laughed.

"Normally I would say okay, but he is different now, and I can't promise he will pay," I said with a chuckle.

"I can't promise he will go home with the same nuts he arrives with," Kate stated with a crooked smile.

"How is he doing back on the force?" I asked Brooklyn since she worked so closely with the police.

"The chief of detectives tried to make Jax and Chase work together to find the shooter, but they both walked out. So they are on the dead man's shift until they learn to take orders."

"How long do you think it will last?" I asked as we piled into the car, and headed into town.

"Those two are some of the most infuriatingly stubborn men. I am ornery, but they take that shit to the next level. They may be the new third shift detectives permanently if they don't get demoted."

"Sounds like the men I remember, only back then they were best friends," I murmured.

"To be honest, I am shocked we are not at their funerals because they murdered each other," Brooklyn chuckled.

"Chase and I are trying this part-time friendship thing where we don't talk about anything serious or anything related to Jax, and we only speak when he comes up for air on his case."

"Oh, that sounds like fun. I want ten non-friend friends," Kate stated sarcastically from the backseat. "You know, the ones you can hump, but not talk to. Those are the best."

"I'm still living a half-life without Jax so there is no humping."

An hour later, we arrived at the first apartment complex on the list and I saw a rat run from the doorway.

"Nope," I nearly yelled. "No way is anyone living here. It is so bad the rats are trying to escape."

Giggles erupted through the car, but I was being serious. I think they were trying way too hard to make me have a good time, but they were my friends, so I would fake it too. There wasn't much that I found funny since my honeymoon.

"Let's go by Tim Horton's. I need coffee if I am going to be doing this all day," I spoke up and they both agreed.

Hours later, I was out of coffee and we had driven all over the city as we crossed off address after address from Queens to the Bronx, and from Brooklyn to SoHo.

"Let's get some lunch," I spoke up as I texted Chase and we headed back to upper Manhattan to meet him.

Chase was waiting at the restaurant when we arrived at the Cafeteria. I loved this place with their light ambience and banana split waffles. We walked inside and sat at the white table and chairs next to the closed garage bay doors that showed us the street view.

I immediately picked up Chelle from her high chair and lifted her in the air. Her laughter was infectious and soon we were all giggling along with her.

"Who is the prettiest girl?" I asked and she pulled my hair.

"Come on, Candy, no need for everyone to know how gorgeous I am," Kate spoke up with laughter.

"That's right, you will always be prettier than Aunt Kate," I stated as I lifted her in the air again and she giggled.

"You look good with a baby," Chase spoke up and I put her back in her high chair.

"I look good because it is someone else's baby. I still get my beauty sleep," I stated with a laugh and Chase reached over and put his hand on mine.

"You have always been gorgeous to me."

"Thank you," I whispered as I nervously pulled my hand away and sat down. The waiter came and we ordered our food.

"How is the house hunting going?" Chase asked as the food was delivered.

"There are better housing options in the poor parts of third world countries after an earthquake, mudslide, and volcanic eruption." I replied.

"Sounds like you are really finding winners there. I found a little place I might take if you want to move in with me, or the offer still stands to run away with me. I will make you waffles every morning," Chase stated and my eyes locked on his.

Was this a set up to get me to move out?

"My dad is paying for everything, and I won't waste his money on a place unless I feel it is needed. Besides, I like spending time with my dad and Michelle." I replied without looking up at anyone.

"Didn't you just release another book? Where the hell is your money?" Brooklyn asked and I knew I should have kept my mouth shut.

"We don't get that much money," I responded, but Brooklyn wasn't buying it. "Wasn't that great of a story because my heart just wasn't in it. Not even enough to put down a deposit." I tried to stop it there, but now they all stared.

"It is still in Jax's bank account," I sighed and everyone looked at me in shock. "The bank said that since we were legally married, I needed divorce or separation papers to remove my name. Or Jax has to be with me or give consent to remove it. It is a specific policy with our account or something. I didn't really understand it. So, instead of calling him, I just let it go and my dad has been paying for my food and stuff. I plan to just change the direct deposit when I find the time."

"Jax gave you the divorce papers, didn't he?" Brooklyn asked and I nodded. "And?"

"I haven't opened them."

Their eyes seemed to look at me for more information as their mouths hung open until Chelle picked up a piece of my waffle and threw it, hitting Chase in the cheek. We all erupted into laughter as whipped cream slid down his face.

As we continued eating, the sun hit me in a manner in which I felt forced to look up. I swallowed down an uneasy feeling and grabbed Brooklyn's knee and forced her to look out the windows.

"I don't know him, but he is here for one of us," she spoke softly as she texted Mark under the table. Chase turned around and his face fell.

"I will be right back. It's a work thing," Chase whispered as he sat his napkin down and smiled at Chelle. Then the man with black hair and a goatee standing in a leather jacket stood where the street split and followed Chase's movements as the sun bounced off his gun on his hip. He didn't look like any cop I had ever seen.

I was intoxicated with memorizing his face in case something bad happened, but a clicking sound pulled me from my trance.

"What are you doing?" I asked. Brooklyn had her phone out and took his photo without even hiding it.

"Taking his photo. If that man steps out of line, I will make sure my office fries him." She then texted the photo to her father and Mark who both knew about criminals in their own way.

"Hide the phone. What if he sees you?"

Brooklyn huffed out a breath and rolled her eyes.

"Men like him only have their eye on the prize and right now it is Chase. I could take off all my clothes and dance on the table and he would still be staring Chase down," she replied, but I didn't like the answer.

I tried to follow their conversation, but there were no hand movements or body language to help me decipher any of it.

"Give me your phone," I requested and took Brooklyn's phone. I blew up the photo. I knew his face. I saw it in the garage when he shot my husband, but I couldn't be positive, because of the sun, that this was the same man.

But it just had to be the same one.

"Tell us the truth about the money," Kate murmured quickly as Chase looked like he was coming back.

"It's nothing," I replied and put away the phone. It couldn't be him because he was working with Chase.

"Bullshit, spill it or I will have Brooklyn fold you into a pretzel. You know she can, and then I will salt your ass and stick you in an oven till you tell us."

"That is a twisted threat, but if you really want to know, then I can tell you it is because it makes it real. I got used to sleeping alone with Chase. The odd hours, eating dinner alone, and the inability to call when I needed something was all part of the NYPD package. I know how to be alone and love one of them, but if I take my name off his bank account, there is nothing left tying us together."

"Sweetheart, you made this decision on your own. If you want your husband back, you have to decide he is what you want and fight for him. You hurt him over and over again. Hell, I love you and don't know if I could forgive you," Brooklyn spoke in a sing song tone, smiling at Chelle, as if talking to her.

"I know, but I am not ready to admit this is more than just him working late," I replied in a rush. "I can't live in denial forever, but to admit that I lost my best friend, my soulmate, and my heart, is not something I am ready for. I decided to walk away, but it doesn't change that I miss him."

"I love you, and am your best-bitchy-friend. Let's start with reminding you that you love me. Because you may not love me when I am done," Kate started.

"You, my friend, are a dumbass, and I mean that with a capital A-S-S. You think you had the perfect life with Chase. You became a best-seller and kick started a better career by signing with a great publisher who doesn't make you want to claw your eyes out from staring at your laptop non-stop. You were in a relationship since damn near birth and you loved him, but you were not in love with him, and life was not perfect."

Kate took a deep breath as Brooklyn nudged her to tell her to be quiet, but I was waiting to hear where she went with this.

"You fell into bed with Jax and rode his lightning. Score one for killer orgasms that make you feel more than the erotic strum that flows through you, but it scared the hell out of you. Then you do the next dumb ass thing and ran away, but you were miserable without him."

I clenched my fist on the table as she continued recapping my life.

"You hide your pain from the world, but those of us who can cut through your bullshit can see it. You came back here after you grieved and felt the actual pain you had been hiding from. You say it was for work, but when you had the option to go home, you didn't. You chose Jax and you both had a chance to have a real life, but you ran from him three more times," Kate added to it by putting three fingers in my face, and counting them.

"I hope you have a point," I growled as this rehash of my life was making me want to leave.

"With Chase, you thought you were in love, and it didn't hurt as bad. With Jax, you felt the love, that burning need to be with him, and love him. You lost him because you are scared it will hurt in the end. That is no way to live your life. You are not made of glass; you will not shatter if you fall. Besides we are here with you. I know you love him, but darling, he is already gone because you couldn't pull your head out of your ass. Now, Jax is gone, and you are stuck with Chase's shadow hanging over you while you try to see him as he was and not as he is."

"You are a bitch, Kate," I bellowed as I stood up and took Chelle to the bathroom to clean her up. Chase was coming in the door as I rushed past him.

"Candy," Brooklyn called out as I sat Chelle on the sink and helped her wash her hands as tears fell down my cheeks. "You don't know that he is gone for good, but you know you are. Each day you are gone and don't talk to him puts another mile between the two of you. I once let Mark go, when he kept something from me, but in the end, he gave me more happiness than anger so I overlooked it."

"Just go," I replied and Chelle turned and washed my face with foam soap as she giggled. Before Brooklyn was out the door, Kate came flying in and pushed me away from Chelle as Brooklyn went to finish washing her.

Kate pushed me near a wall and squatted as she held her arms out. She looked like she was about to fart or play football. It could go either way with her.

"What are you doing?" I asked as she was blocking the way out. "I think you forgot to take your meds today."

"I am the Hugging Hero: hug me willingly or I will force you to feel my comfort."

Kate reminded me of a silly superhero and made me laugh through my cries. I wiped a tear and she stood back up and walked over to me and wrapped her arms around me forcing me to hug her. Chelle clapped with Brooklyn in the background and I laughed at them both.

"Life sucks darlin'," Kate whispered in my ear. "I want to remove both Chase and Jaxson's balls, but you might want kids one day so this is one-time free pass. But when they do screw up again, they will be singing soprano and be missing their sperm mixers. Now decide if you are done running, pick the partner you want, and fight for your right to live. I hate seeing you sad. You hide it well except in your eyes."

As soon as I hugged her back, I heard her lips start beat boxing. I rolled my eyes because here came the Kate that always acted a fool to make people smile

> "All we want to do is slide on their ride,
> and abide by their sex drive.
> I know I want to slide on his ride
> until he is inside my landslide.
> He needs to decide if he wants me bedside

before he collides with my backside.
Who cares if he is unqualified
as long as he leaves me satisfied."

"Kate, don't quit your day job," I laughed and she held out her hand. "What?"

"She thinks she is Fifty Cent and wants her money," Brooklyn laughed and Chelle clapped. Kate took a sarcastic bow. I didn't know how to stop running from life. I wasn't sure how to pick my husband, but I knew with those two women in my life, I was going to be just fine.

Chapter 18

We all had tears of laughter by the time lunch was over as Kate had to sing her song for Chase too. I knew she didn't mean to hurt me, but everything she said was true and that's what was so painful. I just needed to swallow it at this point and move on.

I had had more food than I could possibly stomach and was still curious about who the man on the street was, but Chase wasn't saying a word about it. During lunch, I had cried, I had laughed, and had a good time.

I had a typical first date with three girls and Chase.

"Hey Candy," Chase called out as he was putting Chelle in the car.

"Yeah," I yelled back and walked over to his car. "What's up?"

"I know you and Jax split, and wanted to see if you were up for a date?"

"I don't know, Chase," I whispered.

Chase took my hips and placed me up against the car, then took my head in his hands and placed his lips on mine. I was instantly intoxicated. It had been months since I felt needed, and welcomed it.

I laced my thumbs into his belt loops as I pulled his hardening length up against my stomach. I moaned as he tugged my hair and deepened the kiss.

As his tongue grazed mine, Kate's voice was loud enough to pull me out of my reminiscent fog.

"Do you kiss your mother with that mouth after slobbering on women," she spoke with a smile as Brooklyn chuckled.

"Let me take you out properly with flowers, and breakfast. Give me a chance to make you like me again," Chase whispered in my ear, but Kate heard and answered for me as heat rushed my cheeks.

"She will go, if you are paying and Brooklyn and I get to come, but do not think you are getting a foursome. I ride Eddie's lightning hourly and don't need anymore. Also, I reserve the right to refuse future dates if you don't pick up the tab or if you break any of my five bazillion rules."

I rolled my eyes with a smile and looked at Chase.

"I guess so," I stated without any assurances because it felt a little off. "How about I call you," I offered, as I pulled away to walk off.

"I'll email you my rules, should only take a few months to memorize them. Don't forget my girl here is married so no hanky panky, only over the jeans cock rubs. Hope that is not a deal breaker," Kate called out as we walked away.

"What is wrong with you?" I asked with a laugh.

"Funny or not, my ass leaves a lasting impression," she stated with a grin as we climbed in the SUV and drove off.

By the next weekend, Chase had failed Kate's pop quiz, so she swore I couldn't go on a date with him. I merely laughed because his failures would make her think of new rules to email him. Having her and Brooklyn around really helped me stay sane.

Saturday came and we went to nine more apartment complexes. Each one worse than the last. Neither Kate nor I would ever find a place like this.

"There is only one more and it is a sub-let," I spoke up, exhaustion setting in.

"I love you, girl, but for the last one, do you care if I sit in the car and wait? My feet are killing me," Kate spoke up and I saw both her and Brooklyn were worn out. We had been at this all day.

"I will go up. If it is worth seeing, I will come back and get you. This area is not too bad anyway so I might actually want a place to live here," I spoke up and Brooklyn and Kate shared a smirk through the rearview mirror.

I had known house shopping was a trick.

I plugged in the rest of the address and Brooklyn drove Mark's SUV to our destination. As we pulled up, I noticed it was a familiar building and I opened the door to get out. I looked up at the black high-rise and knew this place, but couldn't place it.

I turned back around as Brooklyn rolled down the window.

"Hey let's let this one go. Just get back in the car," she stated, but I held my hands up to tell her to stay in the car and wait. "I am serious!" she shouted and I went to the door and buzzed to get inside.

I walked down the beige hallway and pressed the button for the manager.

"Hello, sir I am here about the sublet," I said. He smiled and handed me a form to fill out. My phone would not stop ringing the whole time I was filling it out. "Sorry about the calls," I murmured my apologies to the manager.

"I think they are home, but if not, here is the key. 7th floor. They move out on the 13th. The first two weeks are covered and then the first full month's rent is due on the first."

I thanked him and headed to the elevator. I tried to remember the place, but I knew I had never been inside here. Maybe I had seen it in passing. I was born and raised in New York so I had seen it all.

I went up to the 7th floor when my phone chimed with a text from Brooklyn.

"GET OUT NOW! LET'S GO DRINKING!!!!!"

I ignored it, but then another came in from Kate.

"ABORT MISSION, REPEAT ABORT MISSION. IT IS TIME TO KARAOKE."

I didn't know what their deal was, but I was at least going to see the place. I wondered if someone got murdered here, with Brooklyn's job and their constant calls.

Brooklyn did know about who died where by working in the DA's office, but this was New York City. Everywhere you stepped was once a place where someone died. I took a deep breath and let the thought roll away. I walked down to the door and knocked as my phone sounded again. I lifted my phone up and glanced at it.

"EVACUATE THE AREA! DANGER, MRS. ROBINSON!"

Kate had sent another message, but I cleared it and put my phone in my purse. Then, as I knocked again, my phone immediately started ringing and I pulled it out again and answered.

"Brook, seriously give me five minutes," I chided as I looked up, only to be graced with the green eyes and long blond hair of the beautifully tanned Vanessa as the door opened.

"Don't do it, Candice," Brooklyn shouted through the phone. "Don't make me come up there."

"Vanessa," I spoke out loud.

Fuck, I had become the same doorknocker I feared.

"Shit, come on Kate," I heard Brooklyn say through the phone as I ended the call and dropped it into my purse.

"Candice, um hi," she replied and I took in her nervous stance. "How have you been?"

"Umm," I replied getting my thoughts together. "Fine, how have you been?" I asked and she tilted her head.

"Is there something I can do for you?"

"I – um- I-," I stuttered and had no words.

"How did you find us?" She asked, as I tripped over not wanting to shout profanities and rip her hair out.

"Us?" I asked and then Jax rounded the corner and put his hands on her hips pulling her into him.

I swallowed the smile I had been faking as nausea set in.

"Candice." His words froze as we seemed to drink each other in, then when I said nothing, he asked, "What are you doing here?"

"I um..." My words were frozen and my brain stopped working as I watched his grip tighten slightly on her hips. The elevator chimed and Brooklyn and Kate walked up to me.

"Hey, Monroe," Brooklyn called out and he nodded. Kate waved as I looked between Brooklyn and Jax. Fury enveloped my thoughts as I saw that Brooklyn and Kate were not shocked he was here with her.

"What are you lovely ladies doing today?" Jax asked, being the gentleman he always was. Everything my dad had said about thinking first, being more mature, and not running away, went out the window when I saw my husband with another woman.

"Saying goodbye," I spoke up and everyone looked at me. "I came to say I will mail in the divorce papers as soon as I get settled since you obviously have a whore in your life."

"Candice, don't call her that," Jax sneered and I stared into the grey eyes I once knew, but were not familiar anymore.

"I will call her whatever I want because she is fucking my husband!"

"You didn't want him, remember?" Vanessa called out and I went to hit her when Kate grabbed my arm and Vanessa hid behind Jax.

"Candice," Brooklyn called out as I finally turned to walk away.

"You knew," I growled as everyone watched me.

"Candice, there was no need to hurt you," Brooklyn replied as she and Kate walked toward me. Jax stepped out into the hallway and watched as every Band-Aid I had put over my heart went up in flames.

"Candice, don't act hurt now. You left me, remember?" Jax spoke with nothing but disdain for me. He was still hurt or extremely pissed.

"Forgive me for being upset I took my 'thou shalt not commit adultery' vows seriously," I shrieked as I tried to put a lid on the explosion of emotion that was brewing beneath the surface.

"That's the Ten Commandments," Vanessa called out, and I went to rip her hair out when Kate got in my way again.

"Fuck you! I said my vows before God that we were going to stay together for better or worse. Yeah, it was worse, but I did not agree to stay until a new flavor comes along or when things got hard. I said till death do us part," I yelled and Jax cursed under his breath.

"You were not some lamb being led to slaughter. You left me four times. Three strikes and you are out at the old ball game, and I still gave you one more shot, then you left all on your own. No more at bats. The game is over. You chose this."

"Well, thank God. I don't need your diamond plates anymore," I spit out as I pulled my rings off and threw them at him.

Fucking baseball analogies suck.

"Candice, one day you will realize that I wasn't the bad guy here," Jax stated as he let out a sigh and ran his hand through his hair. I noticed he was still wearing the silver wedding band I had placed on his finger and it gutted me. I had to get the hell out of there before I was on my knees begging him to make the pain go away. "I will always care-," I cut him off.

"I have to pack," I called out as I pushed the elevator button and shot a nasty look toward Brooklyn and Kate who played bodyguard to Vanessa. "I am going to catch a cab."

"I'm sorry, Candice, but don't put me in the middle. We are friends with you both, so I haven't talked to him about you and I don't talk to you about him," Brooklyn called out as she stepped forward.

"You know; I don't know what is worse. Him fucking his Barbie whore, or you hiding it from me," I shouted as anger rolled into a saddened rage.

"Damn it, Candice, she is not my whore. She is my fiancé."

"She is your what?" I asked as I was sure I heard that wrong.

"I'm going to be his wife," Vanessa stated as she stepped over to him.

"I'm sorry, I must not have heard you right," I spoke again as I stepped over toward Vanessa. "Move," I demanded Brooklyn and Kate get out of my way. They stepped aside and Vanessa stared at me.

"I'm his- um- you know – bride to be," she replied nervously as I stepped closer.

"No, bitch, you see, I am his wife," I went nose to nose with her and Jax tried to slide an arm in between us and I slapped his hand away. "Listen to me, you home wrecking, thunder stealing, taste my rainbow cunt. You don't know me. You remember what happened to Christina? That was nothing. I would gut you like a fish and drown you in your own blood as if it were a day at the spa. Don't fuck with me, and get away from men that are not yours," I seethed.

Silence fell around us until the sound of paper crinkling had everyone turning their heads. Kate was sliding her Skittles into her purse. I rolled my eyes at her.

"What, I am not the taste the rainbow cunt, I merely love Skittles," Kate stated in defense.

"Read the annulment papers, Candice," Jax said as he put himself between Vanessa and myself. "I told you I wouldn't wait for you, and things happened."

"I fucking hate you," I called out to Jax as Vanessa hurried back inside the apartment. Nausea swirled in my belly and I did everything I could to keep from puking. The tremors had begun and I needed to go.

"I love you Candy, but-," Jax started, but I walked to the door as the elevator still hadn't come.

"Doesn't even matter anymore," I murmured as I hit the door to the stairs, climbing down. I nearly sprinted out of the apartment complex and into the street.

The leather man was standing directly across the street and leering at me when I hit the sidewalk to hail a cab. I walked back and forth as he followed my path. It freaked me out so bad that I stepped out in traffic and stopped a cab that was just pulling away from the sidewalk. I opened the back door and told the man in the cab to slide over.

"I will pay your fare if you let me ride with you. I need to get away," I pleaded and he immediately accepted. "What is your name?" I asked as I slid into the seat beside him.

"My friends call me RJ."

Chapter 19

"Hi RJ, I'm Candice, but everyone calls me Candy. Thanks again for letting me ride with you." I stated as I struggled to calm down and get my phone out of my purse to call my dad.

The lines had blurred as to what was worse. The betrayal from Brooklyn not telling me my husband was living with another woman, or the fact that Jax stayed with her when, deep down, I had hoped my leaving would somehow fix everything.

"You okay? You seem frazzled," RJ asked. It was sweet to see someone showing concern for a stranger as his green eyes seemed to glimmer at me.

"Yeah, I just learned that not everything is as it seems and no one is who they are."

I picked up my phone and called my dad. He would protest and yell, but going to California was good for me until I had to come home, so maybe distance is what I needed.

"Dad," I spoke softly when he answered the phone. "Are you home? Because we need to talk."

After hanging up with my dad, I realized I never gave the driver the address.

"After his stop, I need to go to Elizabeth, New Jersey, please."

"That is a coincidence," RJ stated, and I shot him a questioning look. "I am headed to Newark to handle some flower arrangements. I just got a new shipment in of a specific genus flower called the forget me not."

"Driver, take us to her locations first. Seems her business is pressing where mine is not," RJ stated with a sly grin and I smiled back with a nod to say thank you.

"Why is it named that? Do they use it to remember?"

"A German folklore said the flower called out, 'Forget me not, O'Lord' when it was being created, and God gave it that name. There is one other legend that is similar, but it pertains to the name being about the color. You see, a forget me not is a specific shade of blue," RJ explained, as though he was remembering something fond, a soft smile gracing his lips.

"I never knew that. It is interesting to me that the flower would beg to be remembered, but the color blue is common and flowers are shared every day."

"It is the specific flower that is forgotten. It grows wild and is all over, but no one pays attention to it. They don't give it the same love they would give to a rose. More importantly, the blue it wears is an armor, it hides its pain. When someone with cobalt eyes is in pain and their eyes dilate from the rush of adrenaline, you can look into their eyes and for one fleeting second, you can see those beautiful light blue and silver strands that scream 'forget me not.' I can see it in your eyes right now."

"If it is okay, can we ride in silence? It has been a hell of a day." I let out a sigh as I leaned my head back and closed my eyes.

I felt something graze my hand and looked down to see a business card. I took it and looked at it. It was odd; there was no business name, only the outline of a little blue flower and a beveled phone number. I looked over at RJ in question.

"Please, keep my number and let me repay you for the ride with a drink when you are feeling up to it," RJ smiled.

"I appreciate the offer, but I don't really know you to go alone with you somewhere. If the cab driver wasn't here, you wouldn't be here either," I replied softly. In all honesty, he could have been Chris Pine laying butt naked in the backseat with grapes, saying things like 'let me massage you,' and I would still be in my I-hate-everyone funk and turn him away.

Why did being near Jax for ten seconds make me hate everyone, including myself?

"Why don't you bring some of your girlfriends along with you so you feel safe. Then I can repay you, and all of us can take your mind off whatever is bothering you."

I shrugged my shoulders and looked at his card as he began speaking again.

"My mom used to say, if something is weighing on you, then go watch something worse and you will be grateful for the minor issue you started with." There was a silent pause as I looked out my window. "Isn't the sunset over the Brooklyn Bridge the most beautiful thing you have ever seen? It looks like the bridge is bleeding from the red in the sky," RJ asked and I nodded my agreement as I immediately thought of Brooklyn.

"You know, I have a friend named after this bridge. She is always out here talking to the stars, and pacing the bridge when she needs time away," I whispered as I thought about how much we had in common.

Both our moms died when we were young. We both fell in love with men at the NYPD, but she was tougher than me and blew through roadblocks like an out of control train when something wasn't going her way. She was stronger than me. While I don't know what happened before I came along, I know that it seemed everyone was defensive of her. She hid a huge secret from me, and I wanted to hate her, but instead I felt hurt.

"You should invite her to get drinks with us," RJ offered, as we pulled up outside my dad's house. RJ got out of the cab and opened my door. He held out his hand for me to take and I felt like Julia Roberts in Pretty Woman, except I was wearing jeans and a tank top with a cropped cardigan from the chill that seemed to be in the air.

"Just drinks, and nothing more?" I asked as I took in his expensive clothes that said he was more than a florist.

"Just a way of you saying thank you for sharing the cab," RJ smiled. It might be nice to step out of my life for a night and go out with him. Ninja Brooklyn would have to come, because even though I wanted to throat punch her right now, she made me feel safe around others.

"It would have to be soon. I plan to move away from here as quickly as possible," I murmured, as I made a mental note to remember to sign the papers.

"Tomorrow is booked. I have this cutting edge meeting, so how about next Saturday night?" RJ retorted with a smirk.

"It's Brooklyn's birthday on Saturday-," I replied, remembering that Jax and Vanessa would most likely be at her birthday brunch her dad put together.

"That is perfect. I can take you both out to celebrate that she made it another year."

"Okay it is a non-date date," I replied with a smile.

"Michelle," I called out and little footsteps came running from the kitchen into the large foyer.

"Any," Chelle called out her version of my name and held her chubby little arms out for me. Her green eyes glistened with mischief as I lifted her off the ground and spun her in the air. She laughed and the wind blew her blond curls away from her face.

"You hungry?" My dad asked as he swallowed pills down in the arched doorway.

"No, I think we should talk," I said with a smile on my face.

"It sounds bad, but you look happy so it must not be too bad."

"That is because Chelle is an angel who can take away anything negative. Aren't you an angel?" I asked as I put her down and she started running away for me to catch her.

"Come into the kitchen then, and let's hear what you have done this time," my dad spoke sarcastically.

"Why do you always think I am the one who did something?"

"Because I know you," my dad smiled and I walked through the archway into the black kitchen with my hands on my hips giving him the 'yeah-right' stance. "Jax called right after you did and wanted to know where you were moving to," my dad finally confessed.

"Dad-," I started, but he turned his back to me and started cutting tomatoes for a large pot of sauce he was making for lasagna.

"I have decided to move," I whispered and my dad turned and looked at me. It was a father-daughter stare down, but I wasn't caving. "It's not running away if I make a plan to go."

"What made you decide to leave?" My dad asked as confidence laced his words.

"Nothing, it is just time I get out of the city."

"You are the worst liar in the world," he declared as Chase walked around the corner and agreed.

"Fine! I don't want to be in the same place where my husband is with someone else. My skin crawls with thoughts of him touching her and I will never see that if I am gone. I want to go and start over."

"Candy, you need to talk to your husband. Months ago, you couldn't even stand up and say his name. Now, you are so full of rage and yet you don't have a clue what is going on with him," my dad replied.

"I don't care what is going on with him," I lied and both Chase and my dad shot me that look that told me they knew I was lying.

"Candice, if that is true, then start over with me. I have been begging. Let me take you out tonight and if you don't have fun, I will leave you alone," Chase offered.

"You are not moving anywhere until you talk to your husband or I will fly into whatever airport is closest to you and take a belt to your butt like I should have done years ago! Then, when you can finally sit down again, I will blister your ass again just before I disown you and you will no longer be my daughter," my dad shouted.

"Dad," I started to defend myself and he stopped listening.

"I have spoken, and you will respect what I say because I am your dad. Now make plans, go with Chase and have a fun time. Get a drink, you look like you need it."

I wanted to roll my eyes, but it would just be an additional loss because he had won the conversation.

"I am still moving, but I can take a few weeks to find a place and make sure it's what I want to do," I huffed, like a spoiled child, and turned to walk to the front door.

"Any," Chelle yelled out as I got to the door. She was running for me, but she stumbled and fell. I rushed over to her as tears filled her eyes.

"You are my tough girl," I whispered as she stood up and hugged me. I embraced her and lifted her as I stood. "You are my little tank. No boo-boo is going to get tears from you." She dried up her tears and stuck her finger in her mouth, chewing on it as Chase walked around the corner.

"She okay?" he asked and I nodded as I coddled her. "Candy, come out with me and have one drink. Even if it is not a date, you seem like you could use a few minutes to relax. So come have a drink with me, what could it hurt?"

"I don't know."

Chapter 20

"You can do this," I told myself as I looked in the mirror at the blond tips I was sporting, and the blue eyes that looked like I hadn't slept in a week. I really hadn't slept in a week since we made these plans and I was stuck thinking about my husband every night with Vanessa.

The faded splotchy make up was so attractive that I washed my face so he didn't think I was applying to clown school. "Tonight is like riding a bike that has been in storage."

I pushed up my breasts in my bra so I had some cleavage showing from the red spring dress I was wearing. Then I walked out of the bathroom to see that Chase had lit candles all over the white end tables and counter tops from a white stone studio apartment he was staying in. I didn't see him right away so I dropped my purse on his brown couch and walked around.

As butterflies took root in my stomach, I walked toward the giant four poster cherry oak bed.

"Candy," Chase called my name as I held onto one of the posts. "What are you doing over there?" He asked from the kitchen and I gave him a half-smile. He walked over to the bed and stared at me as I gripped the pole.

"Babe, I wanted to go get a drink with you. I didn't ask you to meet me here to do anything you don't want to do," Chase whispered as he sat on the bed.

"What tells you I don't want to?" I murmured as I found a spot to stare at on his bed and felt my palms turn sweaty.

"You are pale as a ghost. You are shaking like you did the first time you ever let me see you naked. And because you can't even look at me."

"I'm scared. My heart is nervous," I spoke up.

"Candy, it's me. You and I have been through so much that you should always feel comfortable with me."

"When I first saw you in the church, my first reaction was my prayers had been answered because you were alive. Then I wanted to beat the crap out of you."

"And now?" Chase asked.

"I love him. I force myself to hate him for moving on so easily. I make myself hate you for what you did. I am so exhausted from being angry that I don't want to feel anything anymore. The worst part of it all is having to force the hate that I feel all the time. Because we have history and because I love you both like I do, I am not even mad. I forgave you the minute you told me what was going on. It was like a reflex, but you see, that is not normal. Dying and returning doesn't happen without paying some type of cost, and it cost you me."

"Candice, do you want me in this bed tonight, or him?" Chase asked and I didn't want to give him an honest answer because that would hurt him.

"You," I lied and he scooted back on the bed, leaning back as the pillows propped him up, and he looked at me with his arms crossed.

"That was the biggest lie you have ever told," Chase smiled at my failed attempt to keep from hurting anyone. "Try again, Candice."

"It doesn't matter who I want in the bed because you are the one in it," I shouted.

"Maybe I want to be the one you want," Chase challenged as he climbed off the bed to face me. "I know what I did was fucked up and I will pay for that every day of my life, but how long are you going to put Jax between us?"

"You put him there when you died," I cried, and it felt like a weight was lifting off of me to feel something other than pain.

"Well, don't hold back, Candy. Tell me how you really feel," Chase instigated.

"This is all your fault. You died, Chase. You faked it in life, but you died inside me. You took something with you when you left and now all I do is run to avoid feeling that again. But I had to heal. Life forced me forward and I couldn't run fast enough to stop it. Then, when I stopped and embraced what was happening, Jax filled a piece of me and now your piece doesn't fit," I gasped as the words were coming faster than my breaths.

"Then you show up and ruin what was supposed to be the best day of my life, and when I wanted space, you show up on my honeymoon, and suddenly you are there, and my marriage was over." I began to cry. "He found her because of your case. They fell in love when I ran because I couldn't breathe without you. You died, and I followed you into hell to watch the man I love be happy with another. I have to hate you, Chase, or I will be numb to the world."

Chase pulled me into his arms and I sobbed.

"Candy, if that is how you feel, then why would you expect me to climb into bed with you?" Chase asked and I took a deep breath.

"You are the only one who wants me," I sobbed. "You are the only one left who loves me."

"Do you want me to take you in this bed and make love to you?" Chase asked, and the rawness of my feelings left me wavering. "Candy, I want you to tell me you want me. When you do, I will take your clothes off, and I will make love to you like we have done a thousand times before, but it will be different and we will go to new places. I will make you forget him, but you have to be able to look me in the eye and tell me you want me to do that."

"I can't," I mouthed. I walked over and grabbed my purse from the couch, and left. I needed some time and distance to think.

I caught a cab and headed to the park where we all grew up. It was going to be hours before dawn, so I didn't have to worry about being bothered by anyone.

Upon arrival, I took in the new sign that said the park was closed from sun down to sun up. The same sign that paid tribute to a man who was waiting for me in an apartment just a few blocks away. I walked over to the swing and dropped my purse in the sand.

I remembered the three little kids who played here. I could still see those boys running circles around me. Those three little kids were inseparable until love got complicated.

I could still see it like a movie feed in my head. The picnics that Jax would take me on when Chase was busy playing soldier with other kids. I remembered when Jax was the one who would kiss my bruises and cuts as Chase told me to be tougher and try harder.

I grew up into the person I was today because of both of them, but even the seven-year-old in me would never have envisioned how screwed up things would one day get.

As I dug my toes into the sand and closed my eyes to listen to the waves crashing into the wall around the lighthouse, I knew it was time to move, but I had to make peace with leaving again. I needed closure from Chase. I needed one perfect night of Candice and Chase, where no one had a husband, and no one chose a job over the other. I wanted to just have a single solitary night where he was mine and I was his, to see if I loved him as deeply as I used to.

So much about him was different now, but I needed to know if my feelings for him are from the past or did I love the current Chase?

Sometimes I couldn't hear my heart and what it wanted over the grief and thoughts in my head. If I go to Chase now and give him myself, either I would want to stay with him or I would want to run, and I needed to know which way my heart went. I needed to open or close the door on us.

Laughter pulled me from my thoughts as the sun crested over the trees in the distance. I stood up from the swing and walked over toward the merry-go-round to see where it was coming from.

Jax had brought Vanessa to my lighthouse. They were laid out on a blanket, cuddling as the waves came in and splashed them. I remembered when he did that with me as a gut wrenching ache formed in my belly. He brought her to Chase's park, my lighthouse, where he proposed to me. Nothing was sacred when it came to our time together.

I had to get away. I needed to feel something other than pain. I needed someone to soothe me. I needed Chase.

Chapter 21

"May I have this dance, Miss Carson?" Chase asked, holding out his hand to me. Michael Bolton sang about lovers who lie as I took his hand and he pulled me to him.

I swayed to the rhythm as he held me close to him. I knew I should apologize for my outburst, but I just couldn't bring myself to do it. I could barely say anything after leaving the park. I lay my head on his chest as he danced us across the hardwood. I closed my eyes and remembered middle school dances and proms when he would be right by my side.

I knew he loved me then and I knew he loved me now. As much as I loved Jax, I couldn't fight that there was something between Chase and I that felt off or unfinished. I loved him, or maybe I loved the memory of us.

Chase spun me out as the final chorus sounded and then brought me back into his arms. I laughed when I lost my footing and stepped on his feet.

"Get on," Chase challenged me.

I stepped up on his shoes as the song changed and Bonnie Raitt now sung about how she couldn't make him love her. I could completely relate with the song playing.

I hadn't danced on Chase's shoes since we were about ten years old and he was teaching me to dance for our first school dance together. It was technically our first date with supervision, and only the rain drops from that night knew it wouldn't be our last.

I held him tightly as he danced for us both. I watched the sun rise in the distance and I really wanted to make a wish. I had never felt the urge to wish like I was right now, but my faith was an empty boat at sea. One that I would never reach or I would drown trying.

"Take me to bed, Chase," I whispered and he hesitated, but then danced us slowly over to the bed. I got the impression he was waiting for me to change my mind, but I was content with my choice in being here with him. "Just hold me?" I asked as we climbed up on the bed and allowed the hours to pass.

"Candy," Chase whispered as we lay on his bed. "I want to be honest with you. I want to tell you that there is more going on than you know, but it is safer for you to be in the dark."

"What are you talking about?" I asked, as my curiosity was piqued and his face told me he was worried.

"I can't tell you what has happened, but if this or my job ever goes bad, I want you to raise my daughter with Jax. Share custody, or whatever, but I want her to grow up with a wonderful mom who would also be a great role model. I want the man who once knew me best to be her dad."

I rolled over to face him. I saw the fear in his eyes and knew that whatever was going on was bad.

"Chase, you are going to be fine. If anyone was going to kill you, it would have been me," I tried to lighten the mood.

"I'm serious, Candy. If anything should happen to me, and my mom and your dad can no longer raise Chelle, I want you and Jax to raise her," Chase whispered as the seriousness of the situation he was facing settled in my core.

"That day won't come, but if it did, it will be like before and I will welcome her with open arms because once upon a time, I was madly in love with her daddy," I said with a smile. "Someone will need to teach her the difference between a frog and a prince."

"As long as she doesn't go kissing too many to find hers," Chase replied with that she-will-never-date tone that my dad always used to use with me.

"Lay down with me." I pulled his shirt to drag him off the pillows and brought him flat on the mattress while I stayed on my side.

"Candice, I have to ask. My heart has to know. Do you think you will ever love me again like you did before?"

I sighed, leaning over and cuddling into him, laying my head on his chest.

"Chase, I do love you. You were my first love, my first real kiss, my first dance, my first everything. I can't say the words you need to hear because we are not the same people that we were. All I can tell you is that I care about you deeply. When I am not hating you," I finished with a smirk.

Chase pulled my hair back and I looked into those green eyes. The ones that screamed love and laughter. They promised a life of being worshipped and having a family. The same ones I thought I would never see again when he was lying in that casket.

"I have to know what kind of illusion kept your skin cold and hard in that coffin?" I asked as my hand ran across his.

"There was an IV running through my jacket, and the chill was the medicine that kept me in a coma until it was over. To be honest, people see what they want to see when they want to see it. If you believe something is real, your brain will believe it to be true."

I leaned up and stared at him. He was everything I wished for, but yet something was just off. I leaned over him and placed my lips on his. He placed his hands on my back, pulling me in closer as I placed one hand on his chest and pushed my body up without my lips leaving his.

I climbed over him as he opened to let me in. He poured the loss, heartache, and love into his kiss as I felt the emotions run into me. I knew how he felt, but I just couldn't return it. Not wholeheartedly.

"Candy Cane," Chase called out and I sat on top of his waist. "Be sure it is me in this bed with you."

"You have always been with me no matter whose bed I am in," I replied and it wasn't a lie. I had carried him with me whether I wanted to or not. "If this was my last night here, wouldn't you want to spend it with me?" I asked, not giving away that I was leaving.

Chase nodded as I pulled my dress over my head and threw it to the floor as Chase rolled me under him. I yanked his shirt off and flung it across the room.

"Candy-," Chase started to say something, but I cut him off.

"Shh, let me give you a good to go with the bad kiss. It has been a long time since I have been able to give you that," I whispered as I placed my fingers over his lips, then brought him down to kiss me. Familiarity flooded me as he deepened the kiss. I used my feet to push his shorts off so there was nothing between us. No clothing, no Jax, no bad people, nothing was allowed between us as we lay there, open and vulnerable in our own ways.

Whitney Houston came on the radio, singing a beautiful melody talking about how she had nothing without the love of her life, and I knew how she felt. I slid my hand across Chase's face and gave him a little smile as he came down and kissed me again.

I kissed him back with everything that I could give him. I held back, as the memories of guns shooting, and caskets plagued my brain, along with the image of him at my wedding. I kept a piece of me reserved as he moved down and kissed my neck.

I turned my head and gave him access as I ran my fingers through his blond hair. His hand came up and brushed the hair off my face as he looked down on me.

"I love you, Candice," he murmured, and I whispered the words I never thought I would say to him again, and mean.

"I love you, Chase." I stopped there. Normally I would have explained that I wasn't in love with him, but I felt like some part of me needed to reserve that at this moment.

Chase reached over to the nightstand and grabbed a condom. I took it from his hand as his head dropped down to my breasts and he sucked my nipple into his mouth. I sucked in a breath as my teeth clenched down on the top of the condom pack.

"You taste exactly like I thought," Chase muttered as he moved to the other breast and my back bowed up. His phrasing caught me off guard, but a flick of the tongue, and words were forgotten. It wasn't electric, but having Chase here like this was intense. He knew just how to work me to have me gripping the bed sheets and mewling like an animal for more.

He started between my breasts and kissed a trail down my body until he came to my bare mound. I pulled the condom wrapper from my teeth as I watched his head disappear between my legs. I felt him blow across my opening as a warm fluid rushed my thighs.

"God, Candice, I have missed you," Chase spoke with a silvery tone just before his tongue slid into my folds and found my clit. I sucked in a breath as my fist grabbed the sheets. I reached up and gripped the pillow above me and clenched it in my hands, his onslaught on my clit speeding up as he rotated licking and sucking. My breasts grew heavy and my now rosy skin broke out in a sweat as I panted and curled my toes.

"Shit," I said, and I could hear a chuckle just before I felt him suck me into his mouth and his finger pushed inside me to find that rough patch that he had known for nearly ten years.

I cried out as his finger grazed that piece of flesh behind my pelvis and he pulled his head up to look at me.

"I need the condom," Chase stated and I had to focus to hand it to him as the palm of his hand was rubbing circles on my clit while he pushed a second finger inside. I panted and pulled the condom out in a rush as I needed to orgasm more than I needed my next breath.

He slowed his invasion into my senses as I reached for his large cock that was like an old familiar friend. I rubbed my finger across the top and stole the moisture, bringing my finger to my mouth and sucking it in as Chase's eyes lit up in surprise.

With his reaction, I guess I really was vanilla.

Then I pulled the tip and rolled the condom down his long hardened length. I had no clue why

I was nervous before because being with him was like just another day in high school.

"If you are hesitant, we don't have to," Chase whispered as he bit down on my nipple, his hands continuing to work me over until I couldn't hold still at all.

"Chase," I cried and he looked at me as though I was made of porcelain and could break while I was a sweaty panting mess. "Please," I begged and he pulled his hand out, leaving me whimpering as he climbed up over me.

I placed my hands on his shoulders and gripped as I felt him at my entrance. I closed my eyes as he pushed in just a little way.

"Look at me, Candy. I need to know you are here with me," Chase said. I grabbed his neck and pulled him down for a kiss that was deep and rushed. I moaned into his mouth as he pulled out and pushed further in.

"Fuck," I said as he pushed all the way inside me.

"I have rarely ever heard you cuss," Chase pointed out the obvious as he stayed completely still inside me. I wasn't fragile or a shy eighteen-year-old girl anymore. He was going slow and patient with me as he had always done, but I was a raging bull in a china shop as my pussy walls vibrated with a need to release some tension.

I wrapped my legs around his waist and rolled until he got the point and allowed me on top. I stared down at him as he looked at me with love in his eyes. I tilted myself back and began my rhythmic flexes in my hips as I drove him up and down my tightened pussy walls.

"God, Candy," Chase gritted through his teeth as he reached up and pulled me down to him. I leaned down, but never altered my pace. He wrapped his hands in my hair and pulled me to his lips. The faster I moved, the harder he kissed me until I was breathless and on the brink of orgasm.

I sat back up and reached behind me to coddle his balls in my hands and his hands went to my hips as he pushed harder into me. He finally saw I wouldn't break and I bit my lip as he pushed into me in a way he had never done before.

"Chase," I called out as I ran my hand down my face and neck till I came to a stop, pulling my ample breasts into my hands. I faintly heard Chase cuss as my pulse was throbbing throughout my body. I threw my head back as my body weakly climaxed, so I put on theatrics for him.

"Candy," Chase said as he struggled to catch his breath and I screamed as if it was the best ever. I then fell over Chase's chest and I tilted my head up to look at him, giving him a weak, but tired smile.

"Candy, that was-" Chase didn't have to say it. I had learned a few things from Jax that I would always carry with me. It wasn't the best sex I had ever had, but I had to wonder if I anticipated too much going into this.

Chase wrapped his arms around me and held me tightly to him as I realized that I wasn't in love with him anymore. *This had been a huge mistake.* The kind of mistake that could fill the Grand Canyon and still need room. I loved Jax, and wanted to cry being held by another man, but I held it in and climbed off of him. I went to clean up, and when I came back, I noticed a scar on his neck that I had never noticed before.

I climbed in the bed and snuggled with Chase, wondering how much hell he had been through to come back to me, and whether or not I was going to have to fake what my heart wanted from here on out.

Chapter 22

The next morning, Chase was in the kitchen making breakfast. I woke up to the most amazing smells in the house. I hadn't smelled home cooking like that since I was in California, and Andrew was cooking it. Jax and I didn't cook from scratch and typically had things like chocolate, strawberries, and whipped cream off each other as dinner.

I stretched, wrapped the bed sheet around me, and went into the kitchen. I saw a phone I didn't recognize and swiped it to see it had a fingerprint lock on it. I wrote it off as a work phone and put it down on the counter.

"Chase, I think we should talk," I began. He turned to look at me, and his eyes seemed to glimmer with happiness, which made this harder.

"What we did was a mistake. I would love to stay friends with you, but I am in love with Jax."

"You left him," Chase pointed out the obvious and I nodded. "You may love him, but it is me you have a future with." Then he set a down plate of strawberry banana crepes and scrambled eggs with bacon, and I had to ask.

"Where did you learn to cook?"

"Part of my cover from a job I pull for a couple months," Chase replied as he bit into a piece of bacon.

"I don't want to hurt you, and I don't know if I will ever get Jax back, but I have healed from the hole you left, and I don't want you in my life like that anymore."

Chase nodded and walked off to the bathroom. It was then that I noticed there were no scars on his back, but I was sure the coroner's report said two of the bullets went straight through him. I suddenly felt out of place being there and was making myself paranoid because of it. I needed him to be the old Chase, but my gut said he would never be that person again. He gathered up my clothes and brought them to me. I took them and went to get dressed.

When I walked out, he was throwing my food in the trash and was very upset.

"I'm sorry, Chase. I didn't know until – I didn't want to hurt you," I begged for understanding.

"It's fine. I got what I wanted last night," he retorted and I couldn't believe how crass he had become. I grabbed my purse and walked out the door.

The following weekend came up fast. I was getting ready to go meet RJ. I still was not talking to Brooklyn, so I asked him to meet me in the city at the Marriott Marquis because I knew they were having some events that would keep it crowded.

I put my hair up in a French twist and put on a sleek black knee length dress. I took in his rich educated demeanor and hoped my clothes were appropriate. I had brought a bag of personal items with me and gotten a room while movers packed up all my things. I still had my house in California, so it only seemed logical to return since my renters were moving out.

My phone buzzed, telling me it was time, and I slid on my black Jimmy Choo's. I went out to the light hallway and followed the dark carpet to the elevator. I pressed the button and took a deep breath. It was just drinks, but yet it felt like a date. I had never been on a date. I was always with Chase or Jax so there was no in between.

The elevator doors opened and RJ stood inside with a smile for me as he looked me over from head to toe. He was wearing a three-piece black suit with a green tie that enhanced his complexion and made his eyes dance in the light.

"What are you doing in the elevator?" I asked as he held out his elbow.

"Would you believe just riding it for the view?"

"No, I wouldn't," I smiled at him and climbed inside.

"I knew you had a room here," RJ spoke sweetly. He really didn't comment on how he knew, and I wasn't sure at this moment I cared.

Butterflies had made a nest in my stomach and I had to keep taking deep breaths. This was all outside my comfort zone. The elevator enclosed us the entire ride down to the bar. I felt constricted when I wasn't. I placed my hand to the base of my throat and tried to force the feeling down.

"You're safe with me," RJ spoke softly. His voice was trusting and calming, but his green eyes spoke volumes of mischief. "I prefer black-haired women," he joked as the elevator doors opened.

My shoes clicked against the white marble floor as we entered into the bar and took a seat in the maroon chairs.

"A White Russian for her, and a Perfect Manhattan for me," RJ ordered when the server came near.

"Okay, now you have to tell me how you knew I was here and what my favorite drink was," I spoke up as his ordering floored me.

"I'm a business man. I try to know everything about a person before we ever have any contact. I did take the liberty to bring you something that I do not know if you will like," RJ stated, as he snapped his fingers.

An employee walked over, in his vest and dress pants, with a tuxedoed calla lily bouquet that had alternating blue and purple forget me nots mixed in.

"This is beautiful," I whispered and RJ seemed to smirk. He was very confident in what he did. Wish I knew what it was that made him that way. I could stand to use a little of whatever it was he had.

"Dance with me," RJ demanded, and I smiled. I didn't feel like he gave people much of a choice. He was domineering and intimidating. I took his open hand and he pulled me to the middle area of the marble floor where there was an opening.

The music started to play Iron and Wines "Flightless Bird American Mouth." The song made no sense to me. Sounded like a bunch of words strung together for no reason, but as RJ spun me across the floor, I seemed to grasp the meaning that lay beneath the words. It made me think of my husband and the what ifs that would always be there.

"I knew you loved lilies from your wedding, but was unaware if they were the right type. Flowers fit every occasion, but only if they are precise with meaning."

No one else was dancing, but the way RJ commanded attention, I barely noticed. He wanted to be the center of my universe and had inserted himself into that position. I was taken back by his boldness to announce how much he knew about me. He acted as though he had been in my shadow and I didn't know whether to be scared or not.

"You are light on your feet," I commented and his eyes seemed to glisten at the compliment. "How do you seem to know everything?"

"Candice, I know more than most because as long as I know everything, I can't get hurt. I apologize if I come off as brazen, but it is better for me this way. I don't know everything though. Want to talk about what had you upset in the cab?"

"Why do you want to know why I was upset?" I asked and he pulled me into him as his left hand cupped mine on his lapel, and his right hand held me tightly on the small of my back. Then he leaned in and placed his ice cold lips to my neck as he placed a light kiss. Then he whispered against me, "I don't know. In truth, I know why you were upset, but want you to tell me. Something about the blue in your eyes doesn't scream to remember you. They are telling me to save you."

"Why would you want to save me?"

"Us meeting was not by coincidence," RJ spoke softly in my ear as the song changed to "When I'm

Gone" by *Joey + Rory*, and my heart felt heavy. Lost were thoughts of conversation as I thought of my mom and how she had run when she got sick.

She never wanted me to see her as weak, but dad had gone after her and made her come home. He kept her alive long enough for me to get to say goodbye. It was the one thing she had taught me. She had showed me how to run. It was the memory that stood out the most.

Then my mind trailed to my husband and his words 'I won't chase you' and I took a deep breath as I tried to keep the tears away. I didn't want him to give up his life to keep chasing, but oh, how I wanted him to come for me.

Like a white knight once more where he takes away all my choices and hard decisions. To be the person I can lean on, and count on to be there every second of every day. I had walked away and told him not to come for me, which is exactly what he did and what I honestly didn't want him to do.

"How the fuck did you get out of jail?" A familiar voice called out across the room, and suddenly our dance came to a stop.

"Candice, you are about to learn something about me you won't like, but I assure you my intent was never to harm you or omit the information you hear," RJ spoke as he turned me in his hands so my back was to him, and placed his hands on my hips.

I looked ahead in the confusion to see my husband wearing his badge around his neck over a black NYPD polo and jeans. His face was bruised, but he seemed like he was fine.

"What are you doing here?" I asked as Jax stared at RJ.

"Candice?" Jax glared over at RJ, then back to me. "Why are you here with him?"

"Are you stalking me now?" I stated sarcastically, as I crossed my arms over my chest and stuck out my hip with full on attitude. "You know that is illegal in all fifty states."

I felt RJ's hands fall away from my hips as he took my hand and led us back to our waiting table. RJ pulled out my chair and I sat down. Then he sat back comfortably in the chair, not at all bothered by what was happening.

"Detective Monroe, did you come to beg for your wife to come home, or just harass her while she is on a date?" RJ spoke vehemently.

"You are on a date with him?" Jax growled. "He murders women."

"Allegedly, Detective Monroe. See, I have never been caught, tried, or convicted. They assume these horrible things about me," RJ replied as his lips turned up, almost as if he was enjoying this game of taunting Jax.

"You murdered women?' I stuttered as I tried to reign in my shock and dismay. "Were you going to hurt me?"

"Candice, I *might* be a killer, but I could never hurt you," RJ confessed as he reached over and placed his hand on mine.

"Don't believe anything he says," Jax grit through his teeth. "Men like him are all the same. They will say whatever it takes to get what they want, but it is all lies."

"You mean, like to have and to hold, for better or worse, in sickness and health, till death do us part?" I retorted, and had to remind myself that our split was supposed to have been mutual and amicable.

"Candice," Jax ran through a hand through his hair as a sign of aggravation. "This is not the time or place."

"I am on a date. Why are you here?"

"I got a call to this location," Jax stated as I finally heard his radio buzzing with chatter.

"You came and saw everything is safe and sound. Now you can go," I stated, as I stood up and placed my hands on my hips.

"You want me to leave you here with him? Are you insane?"

"Detective Monroe, she is in a public place with a room upstairs. At any point in time, she is free to get help, if needed. But the lady has asked you to leave, so I am going to have to ask you to go as well," RJ replied as he stood up and picked up the flowers. He held his hand out for me and I nervously took it. RJ was acting like such a complete gentleman that I couldn't see a murderer in him, until his eyes glared at Jax.

"He gave you forget me nots?" Jax's voice came out gravelly and the vein in his head was throbbing to its own beat. I showed him my flowers and then hugged them to me.

I hesitated as Jax stepped closer. I trembled from the energy surrounding me. This was more than a jealousy thing. Either way, I needed to hold my head high and walk away. I didn't realize this was a date or that RJ was suspected of murder, but I also didn't want to allow Jax to gloat when he had already taken everything I had to give.

"Walk out of the hotel, get back in your truck, drive home, and don't forget to pick up bleach before you dive inside your cum guzzling gutter rat." I took a few steps toward the elevators with RJ, then I turned back for one more shot at Jax. "Oh, get condoms too because bleach only kills 99.99% of what she has."

Chapter 23

"Do you want to fill me in on what is going on?" I asked as RJ and I entered the elevator. I pushed every button on the panel so we stopped on every floor. I was not going to be trapped in a small enclosed sound proof space with a murderer.

As the door closed, RJ turned and looked at me. Before he could answer, we had moved up a floor and the doors opened and an elderly couple came in.

"You and I could be great friends. You see, I have control over something you want and I want something you have." RJ smiled as he reached up and tucked a fallen hair behind my ear.

Three floors passed us by and the elevator was nearly full when I finally asked him.

"What do I want and what do you need?"

RJ sneered and I tried to focus all my energy on keeping my composure as he pulled me off the elevator on my floor. We got to my room and my bones were stiff to the point I was barely moving. My breathing was erratic as I wondered if my last words to Jax were going to be about bleaching vaginas.

I swallowed hard as he took the key from my purse and opened the door. His foot held the door open and he waited for me to walk inside.

"I won't hurt you," RJ spoke softly and my body believed him while my head screamed at me to run away. I closed my eyes and remembered that the gun Jax and Chase had given me was inside, but it wasn't loaded.

I gulped and walked in slowly as RJ followed. I went and set my purse by the open box that was next to my bed. I grabbed the gun and turned to see RJ pouring a drink from a whiskey bottle that was just waiting for us.

"You know that isn't loaded, right?" RJ asked, as he poured a second glass, when a bang sounded on my door.

How the hell did he know everything?

"Candice, open the fucking door!" Jax bellowed and I internally sighed that he was right outside my door.

"Detective Monroe, you overstep your bounds a lot," RJ sneered as he opened the door. I saw Jax and Mark with the hotel security.

"I am not leaving my wife alone with you," Jax yelled.

"Tsk, are you sure she is *still* your wife?" RJ stated in a sing song.

What the hell did that mean?

Mark walked in and took the drink from RJ's hand and placed his hands behind his back. Then they sat RJ on the bed beside where I had sat my purse down.

"What is going on here?" The security personnel demanded to know and I would love to know that as well. RJ's words that he had control over something I wanted left me curious as to what he could mean. He didn't seem to be in control of anything right now.

"I met RJ when I got in a cab with him outside your apartment with Vanessa. We hit it off, he asked me for a drink, and I said yes. The boxes in the room are because I am leaving New York, and

RJ wanted me to join him for a drink before I left. This intrusion into my private life has gone far enough." I declared as I stood up and placed my hands on my hips. "What is your probable cause for stopping RJ?" I asked, taking something that Brooklyn always asked, but I never understood.

Security stepped out into the hallway and were whispering and relaying messages about the situation. I swallowed hard, but held my focus on the two NYPD detectives who had once been family.

"Candy, can I talk to you outside?" Mark asked, but didn't let me answer as he drug me into the hallway and down toward the elevator.

"What the hell are you doing with him?" Mark asked and I shrugged my shoulders. I really didn't know.

"Why do you care?"

"He has been chasing Brooklyn for years. The scar on his shoulder and leg are from her, when he was waiting in her apartment to kill her. This man has killed so many and he leaves them naked and covered in-."

"Forget me nots," I finished Mark's statement as I knew where it was headed. "I know this sounds weird, but I don't think he will hurt me. I get the impression that he is often misunderstood. Maybe he didn't mean to hurt Brooklyn and maybe someone else killed those women," I whispered. I didn't believe what was coming out of my own mouth.

"Jax and I can't leave you in there with him and you know it," Mark retorted as I paced in front of the elevators.

"Jax can go to hell," I challenged and Mark merely shook his head.

"How long are you going to keep doing this?" Mark asked and I paused.

"What am I doing?"

"Your boxes are packed. You are running again. Why does love scare you so bad that you flee the scene as soon as you can?" Mark asked, but I had no answer.

"Mark, I-," I started, but couldn't find the words.

"You love him. I can see it written all over your face," Mark sighed.

"Is it that obvious?" I asked and Mark nodded.

"You should know, before you tell us to walk away, when RJ finds a target, it starts with someone, usually a woman with blue eyes like yours, getting stabbed. He likes to toy with his victims, so he sews up their wounds till they heal and then he tears through the scar tissue to maximize the pain.

"When their time comes near, their skin turns cold and their breaths become shallow. You watch as their soul slowly pulls away from their body, and the pain they go through while they try to cross over. You will go to them, beg and plead for them to fight and live, but because of men like RJ who so easily get inside their heads, they think it is easier to give up, so they do. Then you watch as they struggle for one more last breath until their heart stops beating."

The air around us turned ominous as Mark spoke. I could almost envision my future like that.

"You speak like you have seen it happen, but you have the love of your life, so he must not be any good at catching her," I stated with a hint of sarcasm.

"Before you came along, Brooklyn had died twice from his hand. What do you think it would do to her and Jax if RJ took your life too? What do you think would happen to me and her if she knew I left you here to die? If she knew you were here with him, she would give up her life to keep him from harming you. All of us would, because we all, including Jax, love you."

"I get it, Mark; you are scared for me. Nothing RJ has said has been a lie, and he said he wouldn't hurt me. Now, if you and Jax want to sit outside my door all night, then you go ahead, but I am going in there and I am closing the door. I am going to talk to my date, and have a drink."

I walked off and headed back into my room. RJ looked like he was sporting a new bruise on the side of his head and a busted lip. I squinted my eyes at Jax who had fresh blood on his knuckles.

Mark walked in behind me and un-cuffed RJ. It took Mark and four security personnel to remove Jax from my room as he screamed at me to let him stay.

I walked over to the door and gave them a half-smile and closed the door. I then went and turned on the shower and the fan in the bathroom as I wiggled my finger for RJ to follow.

"Are you going to kill me?" I asked bluntly.

"You are not what I want," RJ replied. "While I would love to look into your eyes as they met the blade of a knife, I can't. I told you, your eyes are begging me to save you. I would get nothing from killing you myself."

"What do you want from me?" I asked as the room filled with steam.

"I know who wants your husband dead and why," RJ stated and I softly gasped. Someone really did want him dead. I knew it, but not being around him every day allowed me to deny it. "You see the new bruises he has. That was from a swinging 2x4. He really should pay better attention because death is everywhere. I can either stop those that are harming your husband or I can help them and take his final breaths away from you." RJ smiled like a Cheshire cat.

"What is it you want from me?" I asked and the answer had been there the whole time.

"Brooklyn," RJ walked up to me and whispered in my ear. "A life for a life. If I get her, you get your husband back, safe and sound. If I don't, then you can bury him next to Chase."

"Chase is dead?" I asked as tears filled my eyes. "But I just saw him," I stuttered.

"Life disappears in the blink of a blue eye," RJ tsked me and smirked. He seemed to enjoy being in control of this situation a little too much.

"Why me?" I rasped out.

"You constantly run from life, so it left you open to run to me. You need me right now. Those you love are still alive because I want to see what you choose. I want to save you from yourself while we play a little game. If you choose neither, they all die."

"How am I supposed to choose?" I asked. RJ merely shook his head and I yelled, "How do you expect me to decide between them?"

"Sweet Candy," RJ started as he pushed that stray hair behind my ear again, and I smacked his hand away. "Careful dear, you wouldn't want to anger me. If you think about it carefully, you already know who to choose. Your husband is living with another woman, isn't he? Didn't Brooklyn keep that information from you? Seems to me like it would be an easy decision, but I will give you time to think about it."

"Wait," I called out in some need to delay him leaving. "What would you choose?" I asked, hoping it would lead me to something more than what I was being given.

"Candy, I would choose myself and they would all die. Cross me once and it is an out at the old ballgame."

"How do you know that Jax or Brooklyn wouldn't kill you?"

"Because, when given the chance, neither pulled the trigger in the right place to end me. As long as I live, so do all their secrets."

Then RJ stepped out of the bathroom. I sank to my knees. I have to choose who lives and dies? I am not God. There was no way for me to choose. I loved them both no matter what had transpired.

"Hope you enjoy California, dear. Your house there is absolutely lovely."

I sucked in a deep breath as he walked out of the hotel room. How could someone so vicious hurt me, but yet never lay a finger on me.

Chapter 24

"Candy, look at me," Jax pleaded. I was now sitting on a bed.

How did I get out of the bathroom?

I looked around at the light walls and darkened carpet to see I was still in my room. "Sweetheart, come back to me."

I turned and fell on my stomach onto the white sheets with an exasperated sigh. Then I heard Jax mutter something and we were all alone as the door clicked shut. He laid down beside me on his belly and stared at me. Our hands laying on the bed side by side and sparking to life without a single touch.

"Talk to me," he begged.

What was I to say?

Do I tell him the truth and allow him to sacrifice himself?

Do I lie and keep it from him so he is unprepared and gets killed?

If I saved him, would anyone ever forgive me when we stood at Chase's, or Brooklyn's, funeral?

How could I live without any of them?

"I can't," I whispered answering my own questions that were rolling through my head.

Jax leaned his pinky finger over onto mine and I closed my eyes as the tiny touch that had me craving every inch of him. I don't remember a time in my life where I didn't love Jax. There wasn't a day that went by that I wasn't with him. If he got the flu, then Chase and I visited him often. When Chase got sick, I stopped by, but spent my time with Jax. How could I have so easily of overlooked the bond I was forming with Jax? How could I have been so scared that I could walk away?

"Candy, it is just you and I in this room. We are the only two people breathing this air. Your heart is slowing to match mine the way you always have when your anxiety speeds up. The quiet breath that we are sharing is becoming softer as my touch soothes you. I know everything about you, so trust that whatever it is, I can know that too."

"You will die," I spoke so softly my words were barely heard over my breaths. Shock had formed over my tears, and kept them from showing as I watched Jax's face turn to concern. His brows furrowed and his gorgeous grey eyes seemed to pulse as adrenaline ran through him with thoughts of the unknown.

"Candy-," Jax started, but I turned my head away from him. The bed rippled as he moved over me. I felt his weight come down over me as my body bowed into the bed. His arms stretched out to match mine and his hands covered mine. "I would lay my body over yours like this to protect you. Do you feel safe?"

I shook my head as his breath on the back of my neck gave me goosebumps. How could I feel safe with him, when he was one of the targets all along. I didn't know if trouble followed me or him, but I know it has been a hell of a ride since Chase got shot.

"Jax-," I murmured, when his weight left my back and he pushed down my body from the hips down. Then I saw his elbows bend and he began picking the bobby pins out of my hair.

"You have such gorgeous hair. You shouldn't keep it up, unless you wanted him to have access to your neck," Jax whispered in my ear as my hair began to fall a piece at a time around my face. "Do you feel me here with you? Can you feel me on top of you? Taking care of you? Protecting you?"

I shook my head again. Only this time it was a lie, and Jax knew it, because my body told him. I felt a rush of heat when he gathered up all my fallen hair into a pony tail and forced me to look into those grey eyes that I wanted to see every morning when I woke up and every night when I went to bed.

I wanted to have children that had his eyes and personality. I wanted them to carry his strength and fearlessness. The only thing I wanted for my future kids was to have Jax as their dad and me as their mom.

"Why her?" I asked, and I heard a sigh. "If you want me to tell you, then you have to tell me."

Then I felt Jax get up, walk over to the desk, and pick up the gun I had set down. He placed it inside the box. Then he gathered up my laptop and placed it inside my messenger bag. He pulled out the manila folder I had been avoiding and set it down on the table.

He leaned on the desk beside the papers as I turned and sat up. He crossed his arms and took a deep breath.

"You left and she was there, trying to be a friend. I realized that I never had to chase her. She was always there when I needed her. She does everything in her power to make sure that I am happy so she can be happy too. I love you, Candice, but she was almost too good to be true when you left."

I stood up and walked over to him. I ran my finger across the folder and sucked in a breath.

"Is she the one you want?"

"No, but she is a great runner-up," Jax whispered. He came around behind me and placed his hands on my hips. "Tell me why you were on a date with RJ."

"I don't know," I replied as I leaned back into him. My eyes didn't leave that folder and I had the impression that Jax wasn't leaving without them signed.

"What did he do to you?" Jax asked and I turned in his grasp to face him.

"He took control; it was scary and thrilling. I danced with him and never thought about running from him because I knew he wouldn't let me," I stated as I heard Jax inhale a sharp breath.

"Is he the one you want?"

"No, he is a shitty runner-up," I chuckled, throwing Jax's words back at him. "He is an evil man, and that is not what I want."

"What did he want, Candy?"

"You," I said quietly, as I pointed my finger into Jax's chest just under the collar bone where he had been shot.

"What does that have to do with you?" Jax asked with his detective demeanor carrying his words across formally as if he wasn't nearly chest to chest with me.

"Nothing," I retorted quickly and Jax tightened his grip on my hips.

"Liar," Jax called out and I leaned up and laid a kiss on his cheek.

"I don't kiss and tell," I replied and Jax let me go. "I am going to go take a shower, and when I come back, you won't be here. If you have any further questions, make an appointment with my legal counsel and we can all talk then."

Then I went into the bathroom and climbed in the shower. I tried to scrub RJ's lips off my hand and neck. I tried to remove his scent from my body. I sobbed on the floor when I could still see him all around me with no one here. His nefariousness lingered all over me as my brain spun with the what ifs of my impending decision.

"Candy," I heard my name and then a loud bang. I covered myself as if a bomb had just exploded. Jax ripped back my shower curtain and looked down on me in the bathtub.

"You should go," I pleaded as the tears wouldn't stop coming.

"For better or worse," Jax replied and stopped the shower and shifted it to the spout to fill up the tub. "Let me in, Candy. I won't hurt you."

"I hate you," I replied and started building a wall between us. "You are the source of every pain I have."

"You don't hate me. You are scared from what your eyes are saying. You want me to leave and let you hate me, but we both know I can't leave you like this."

"I'm fine," I gritted out.

"Candice, you scrubbed your hand until you drew blood," Jax pointed out that I had opened the flesh over my knuckles and my stomach churned as I could still feel RJ there. He barely touched me and yet I felt like I had been skinned and left open to every element.

"I was trying to get clean," I whispered and Jax looked concerned.

"Did you have sex with him?" Jax asked and I shook my head. Then Jax kicked off his shoes and dropped his jeans.

"What are you doing?" I asked as he pulled his shirt up over his head.

"I'm going to help my friend get clean," Jax spoke quickly. "Scoot up and let me in," Jax demanded and I slid up to the front of the tub. He climbed in behind me and pulled me back till I was laying on his chest.

I turned my head to the side and saw the little scar the bullet had left. I flinched at first glance, but then something called to me. I turned around and looked at it closer as the tub was nearly full.

"A water wish," I spoke up, and Jax reached over to turn off the water. "You are my water wish?" I asked, not knowing how to convey what I was trying to say, and from the look on Jax's face, he didn't get it either. Then I trailed my finger over the scar that was in the shape of a rain drop.

I heard Jax suck in a breath as I traced the outline of the tear drop shaped scar. Then, without a thought in my head, I laid back on him with a sigh. I was content with him here and now, so why couldn't I stay that way.

Jessie J's "Flashlight" started singing from his phone on the bathroom floor. I felt him jump and knew it was her. It would always be her. She could make him happy and I would keep him fit with all the running he would have to do.

I climbed out of the tub and put on a robe. I quickly left the room as Jax was calling my name. I went to the desk and opened the folder I didn't want to open. I dripped water all over the papers I didn't want to sign. I separated the two pages and glanced over them.

I got toward the bottom of the first page where the property/assets/notes to file was and I gasped. Then I followed it over to the second page as my heart melted and rage fired through me.

It states:

To Whom it may Concern:

I never turned in the marriage certificate, so legally we are not in need of a divorce or annulment. I didn't want her subjected to any more pain than necessary. I want to make sure she gets everything she deserves. I am leaving my wife: my truck, my house, my bank account, my favorite football jersey, and my favorite Metallica hoodie – she has already taken possession of.

I want her to have everything since I failed at giving her enough to stay. This includes giving her my heart, my soul, and my manhood because without her, I am nothing.

"We're not married?" I nearly yelled at him to cover up the tears that wanted to fall.

_____

Plaintiff,

vs.

_____

Defendant.

CASE NO.: _____

DEPT : _____

DATE OF HEARING: _____

TIME OF HEARING: _____

DECREE OF ANNULMENT

(No Children)

This Decree was submitted (☒ check one) ☒ after a hearing ☒ without a hearing before

the above entitled court, and after a review of the pleadings and papers on file and the testimony

given, if any, this Court finds as follows:

1. That this Court has jurisdiction to grant an annulment because: (☒ check one)

☒ The parties were married in the State of NewYork on (date) _____

☒ The parties were married in (city) _____, (state) _____

on (date) _____. (Name of NewYork resident) _____

has been a resident of the State of NewYork for at least six weeks prior to filing this

action and intends to make New York his/her home for an indefinite period of time.

2. Pregnancy. (☒ check one)

☒ Neither spouse is pregnant.

☒ The following spouse is pregnant: (name of pregnant spouse) _____,

The other spouse (☒ check one) ☒ is / ☒ is not the parent of the unborn child. The

child is due to be born on (date): _____

3. That Plaintiff and Defendant have no minor children in common who are either

biological or adopted.

4. That the Plaintiff or Defendant should be granted a Decree of Annulment for the reasons

set forth in the Complaint or Counterclaim.

5. That any other necessary findings of fact are attached and incorporated herein.

Property/Assests/Notes to File:

To whom it may concern: I never turned in the marriage certificate so legally we are not in need of a

divorce or annulment. I didn't want her subjected to anymore pain than necessary. I want to make sure

she gets everything she deserves. I am leaving my wife, my truck, my house, my bank account, my

favorite football jersey, my favorite Metallica hoodie - that she has already taken possession of.

CASE NO.: _____

DEPT : _____

I want her to have everything since I failed at giving her enough to stay. This includes giving her my

heart, my soul, and my manhood because without her I am nothing.

_____

_____

NOW THEREFORE, IT IS HEREBY ORDERED that the marriage of Plaintiff and

Defendant is hereby declared null and void and of no effect, and each of the parties is restored

to the status of an unmarried person.

IT IS FURTHER ORDERED that (☒ check one)

☒ The wife should have her former or maiden name of

restored.

☒ The wife never changed her name or does not wish to have her former or maiden

name restored.

DATED this _____ day of (month) _____, 20 _____

_____

DISTRICT COURT JUDGE

Respectfully Submitted:

By: **_Jaxson Monroe_**   By: _____

    (Plaintiff's signature)   (Defendant's signature)

(Name) _____   (Name) _____

(Address) _____   (Address) _____

_____

(Telephone) _____   (Telephone) _____

(Email Address) _____   (Email Address) _____

Chapter 25

"You never turned in our marriage certificate?" I growled and read the pages again.

"Candice, I thought it would be easier since we were off to a rocky start to wait, and then you left."

"How can you just give me everything like that when all I wanted was you," I rasped out as I punched the papers on the desk.

"Candy, I loved you, but it wasn't enough. We both knew that."

I wasn't supposed to see him move on. I wasn't supposed to fall deeper for him after reading the annulment papers. I called room service and ordered a bottle of vodka. Straight up alcohol was needed without some garnishment to flavor it. I wanted the raw burn to pour down my throat.

I grabbed my clothes and went into the bathroom to put them on. When I came back out, Jax had done the same, and was texting as a knock sounded on my door. I opened it took the bottle and turned it up before I even shut the door.

"Do you have a drinking problem?" Jax asked as he took a swig and walked over to the window with my bottle.

"I took my vows seriously. They were more than just turning in papers," I whispered. "You took away my choice to be married to you or not from me."

"I'm sorry," Jax spoke softly and I nodded my head, but forgiveness wouldn't come anytime soon.

"I wanted time to work it out in my heart, and I wasn't ready to sign them," I whispered as I looked at him as my heart welled up with all the pain and suffering I had felt for months.

"You would have never been ready," Jax growled as he ran his hand through his hair. Frustration was setting in and I was glad.

"I should have been given a choice, but since I wasn't, how about let's rip off the band aids and be honest about the whole thing."

"Candice, anything I say is going to hurt both of us," Jax stated as he ran his hand through his brown hair again, then he took another drink.

"Take a drink and say it. I have nothing left to lose."

"Candice, alcohol is just a temporary numbing tool. When you are sober, you will feel every word I say," Jax whispered, and I walked over and stood in between his legs as he sat on the bed. I placed the bottle to his lips and tilted the bottle up.

How I wished my lips were the bottle as I watched him suck the clear liquid into his mouth as his eyes glimmered for a fleeting moment.

"Jax, I never meant for any of this," I whispered as he stood up and took another drink before he started to toward the door.

"You never mean for anything, Candice, but you hurt others to avoid feeling any pain yourself. You claim it is because you don't want to hurt anyone, but you hurt everyone around you. You run so you don't have to feel the ache, but we all feel it every time you pack a bag."

"Jax, that is not fair," I screamed. The alcohol was finally invading my core and my body filled with tingles as my body warmed to a desert temperature.

"Fair?" Jax scoffed. "Let's talk about fair," Jax stood up and started to pace, and I knew I had set off a bomb waiting to explode.

"I watched my best friend, my brother, get shot. I buried him and eventually made my peace with it. I fell in love with my best girl. The one who made me want to get up every morning and fight through the bad I see every day to see her smile every night.

"Then, when I thought we had come so far on this journey, when I thought you and I both were ready to have a happily ever after together, I proposed. I made you my wife, only for you to tell me you can't be with me because the friend I lost in the beginning shares the air we breathe. How the fuck is that fair?"

"Jax," I cried out. He walked over to me and placed his hands on my arms as I started to falter my step.

"How is it fair that when I placed my hands on my wife, she said no because she was confused about another man, but the man she is confused about is able to whisk her away easily with a lie on our honeymoon? How is it fair that he crawled right back into your heart and has your trust when I fought for what seems like forever to get a tiny piece of you? How is it fair that when I think you have finally chosen me, you tell me not to chase after you because you were ready to run again."

"I-," I began, but Jax put his finger on my lips, and I sobbed in silence as he took the bottle and gulped it down as I had.

"How is it fair, when I move on with my life and finally stop thinking about you every second of every day, someone calls and says you need me and I come running?"

I grabbed my stomach as pain filled my soul. Even the alcohol couldn't stop the assault on what was left of my heart.

"You said we would be together forever," I gasped through the tears. "No matter what happened, we would always work it out."

"And I meant it, until you told me it was over and I wasn't to come for you anymore. That hurt. Hearing you slept with Chase was even more painful, but seeing you on a date with RJ... that cut me deeper than anything else ever has. Now, after all of that, I don't want to know you," Jax replied as he picked me up off my knees. "I don't want to love you, Candy. I want to punish you the way you punished me. I want you to feel the pain that I felt. The heartache I still have to breathe through day and night."

I wrapped my arms around him and held on tight as I sobbed. I heard the liquid going down his throat and did the best I could to dry my tears. I grabbed the bottle from him and tipped it up until more spilled down my white shirt.

Jax took a step back as I wiped the liquid from my chin, and I saw the gleam in his eye I had seen a million times before. I tipped the bottle back up and missed my lips as the room temperature liquid crashed down over my shirt.

"I am always going to love you, Jax, but I don't know how to stop running."

"Why don't you try running to someone instead of away from someone. Surely someone out there can make you feel safe and loved," Jax suggested, and it was like a knife in the heart.

"You did. You're the one who makes me feel that way. Your scar proves it because it is my water drops. Wonder what would happen if I made a wish on you," I drunkenly replied.

I held out the bottle and Jax stepped forward and took it. He took a drink and held it in his mouth as his lips crashed down on mine. The second my lips opened to him, the warmed alcoholic drink rushed from his mouth to mine.

Jax pulled away to set the bottle down as I struggled, in my impaired abilities, to get my shirt over my head. I felt hands hold my shirt still as my breasts were freed when my bra was pushed down.

The first grazed of his tongue on my nipple had me dropping to the floor and Jax picked me up and carried me over to the desk. He laid me across it and pulled my shirt off. I peeked over the blindfold my shirt made to see him walk over and grab the bottle of vodka. He poured it over my breasts and then his lips sucked my nipples into his mouth.

Jax sat the bottle beside me, and I fought not to wiggle and knock it over. I screamed as he sucked and flicked his tongue on one nipple as his hand unfastened my jeans. I bent my elbows out and grabbed his brown hair and held him over my breasts as he pushed my pants down.

"Candy, how drunk are you?" Jax asked as he pulled back. I pulled off my shirt and climbed off the desk, letting my jeans fall and then pulling off my white silk thong and letting my bra drop. I stood before him naked, and feeling more beautiful than ever with the way he looked at me.

"I'm not drunk enough to do anal, but if you want to dip your cock in vodka, I will suck it clean," I replied with no filter over my words.

"Candy, you are too vanilla for anal, but one day, I'm sure you will love it."

"You think I'm still Vanilla?" I asked and Jax nodded.

"I need to know that you are sober enough to consent to being with me. If you want to stop, we can."

I walked over and pulled on his black belt and opened the button to his jeans. I pushed them down and grabbed the bottle. I poured the rest of the vodka over his long hardened cock and then dropped to my knees.

I was quick to pull him into my mouth before he could notice that I nearly stumbled in my inebriated stated. I tasted vodka and silky flesh as I hollowed my cheeks and began the in and out movements with my head. I took a quick peek up to see his eyes meet mine.

I was so in love with a man who I had hurt, pushed away, and ran away from. I didn't deserve him, but I wanted him. I made a huge mistake letting him go, and now he was with another. I could get rid of her but then he would be forced to be with me instead of choosing me.

I moaned and pulled him deeper into my mouth as I was quick to move up and down his length. I heard a groan as I pulled him to the back of my throat and swallowed. I coddled his balls in my hand and pulled him out of my mouth when my jaw got sore.

Jax looked down on me as I massaged his balls. He pushed the hair from my face and then he slowly dropped down to his knees.

I fell back on the floor as Jax climbed over me and laid his body down on top of mine. He looked up at me and grinned when I tried to grind against him for some kind of friction.

"You want to stop and let me take care of you?" He chuckled when I groaned in frustration.

"Jax," I whimpered and he leaned up over me.

"No foreplay, no love making, no pansy shit. I want to take you and fuck the shit out of you for the way you treated me. Then, on round two, or maybe round, ten I will coddle you and make love to you."

I nodded my approval as if it mattered. I felt him at my entrance as he came down and placed his lips on mine. I opened to that rush of alcohol as his tongue invaded my mouth. I felt his hands push mine above my head as I gave myself over to him.

I kept my hands where he left them as he pulled my knees up and spread them further apart. I felt his teeth on my neck as I turned my head and gave him more access. Gone were RJ's touches of ice. They had been replaced with the fire that Jax leaves in his wake. The winds began to howl against the window and thunder echoed in the background as Jax pushed into me just a fraction.

"I would loosen up," Jax muttered against my skin as I tightened down on him. I tried, but my pussy had a mind of its own, and didn't want to let go. He took his thumb and slid across my clit until I was focused elsewhere and panted with need.

"Ready?" he asked and I gripped the leg of the desk behind me. I nodded my head. He pushed into me, hard and fast. My body wasn't used to it, so it resisted, but then he pulled back a fraction and pushed in again and the resistant walls loosened their grip to allow him in.

I shed a tear out of the corner of my eye as I looked at him, and he took notice.

"Did I hurt you that bad?" he asked as guilt immediately invaded his grey eyes, and I cried softly.

"No, it's not painful," I replied as a rush of air escaped my lungs. "It's just-" I couldn't finish my statement.

"It's just that you are overwhelmed because you love me and it is me inside you where you thought I would never give you this again," Jax asked as he stayed completely still until he knew I was okay.

"Sometimes you knowing me so well sucks," I replied and he pulled out and pushed back in.

"I can think of a few times you screamed that you love it when I know you," he stated with a smile as my body urged him to do more, but the tear had halted his need for an angry fuck and the alcohol seemed to evaporate as we entered our own little world.

My brow broke out with sweat as I pulled my arms down and gripped his shoulders.

"You fit me fucking perfectly," I shouted as he pushed into the hilt again. "You are so deep I can nearly taste you."

"Fuck, Candy, you are going to kill me," he growled.

"What?"

"Between your vanilla attitude, potty mouth, and how tight you are, I am a goner," Jax grit through his teeth as I tightened down on him again as my pussy walls pulsated in rhythm with my heart.

I giggled, but it only lasted a millisecond as he leaned his head down and sucked my nipple into his mouth. I gasped and my back bowed off the floor. I tried to move my hips to get him to move faster, but he always did it his own way.

I pushed my nails into his skin as his tongue and his cock matched rhythm as they assaulted my senses. The smell of Irish spring invaded my nose as sweat broke out across Jax's back and I needed control. I rocked my hips and he rolled with me to let me get on top of him.

I made a silent O as I sat on top of him. I looked down into those grey eyes I loved so much and I saw my storm. I finally saw a glimpse of the love we had lost.

"You okay," Jax asked as my face fell. My mind flashed from what we would be like had we stayed together and where we were headed now and I wanted to cry.

"I am perfect," I lied as I leaned over Jax and the blond ends of my hair fell all around his face. He reached up and moved my hair out of the way so he could watch my face as I slid up and down his hardened cock at my own pace.

I watched as his eyes dilated while I drove us for a while. I went into a fantasy world inside my head where this one moment would fix everything.

I could feel every vein as it pulsated with his heart through my pussy walls. My heart, and his, strummed to a similar beat that kept my movements in sync. Jax reached his hands up and massaged my breasts as I moved a little faster.

I was climbing up the climax cliff fairly quickly, but I didn't want it. I wanted this to last forever. I leaned down and ran my tongue across that water drop scar and heard Jax grit his teeth.

"Shit," Jax murmured as I laid a kiss over his scar. My breasts felt heavy and my skin flourished in a rainbow of pinks. I swallowed my moans as I sat back up to let my head drop back.

Jax's hands went to my hips and he took control as I struggled with the need to come. He pushed into me over and over again as I balled my fists and curled my toes. I bit my lip and looked down on him. I whimpered as I struggled to stay off my orgasm.

"Candy, just let go," Jax commanded.

I shook my head that I was holding out for him, but Jax took one hand and brushed his thumb across my clit as he pushed against that rough patch behind my pelvic bone.

"Jax," I screamed as euphoria ran through me, leaving me undulating in a chaotic pattern as another orgasm showed up on the horizon like a storm hiding under the blanket of night.

Jax rolled me and lifted one leg over his shoulder as he pushed into me again and I felt him swell inside me. I dug my nails in as the second orgasm gripped me and refused to let go until I had felt it from the top of my head to the tips of my toes. My body tensed and felt torn, but like a good Mr.-Clean-Magic-Eraser-type-orgasm, all was right as rain as those tight feels dissipated, leaving behind a relaxed limber body in its place.

Jax leaned over and captured my lips, and I swallowed his groan and he pushed into me hard as he found his release. I wrapped my arms around his neck and kept kissing him until I was breathless and my pussy walls were vibrating him back to life.

"I love you," I whispered and Jax pulled back and looked at me as a tear fell from my eye.

"I know, Candy. I have always known." The next round was much slower as our bodies were not quite ready to say goodbye. Neither was my heart.

Chapter 26

I woke up as the sun bared down through the windows of the hotel room. I turned my head to see Jax was asleep beside me on the bed. I rolled away from him and stood up to look out the window.

The hotel's groundskeepers were picking up the debris from the storm. I grabbed my clothes and started getting dressed when I felt a hand wrap around my ankle.

"Why is it, when you wake up, you are up early and full of smiles, but when I wake you up early, you are not you and I usually get the finger?" Jax asked and I chuckled.

"I am in a great mood and want to get up early when I have been satisfied over and over again the night before. How is your head?"

Jax tried to sit up and grabbed his head as the overabundance of alcohol was hitting him. I walked over to my purse and pulled out a bottle of aspirin. I swallowed two and gave him two.

"So the trick is to fuck you all night and you wake up hyper and happy. Noted."

"What was this?" I asked as I put my shoes back on and looked for my shirt. There was a silent pause in the room that forced me to sit on the bed and wait for the eye contact Jax was avoiding.

"This was a mistake," Jax regretfully announced. I suddenly wondered if this was karma for Chase, because it was exactly what I told him. "I needed information and instead I cheated on Vanessa. I hurt her again, and I swore I wouldn't."

I sighed when I heard his answer. I knew it was coming, but it didn't take the sting away when the words left his mouth. I knew it was goodbye, but hoped my pussy could cast a spell on him to make him overlook my flaws. But like faith, magic doesn't exist.

"I will tell you what you want to know and you can go. This can be our dirty little secret. My flight is at 5pm today anyway. I need to make sure everything is lined up and say goodbye to my dad and Chelle."

"We really messed this up, didn't we?" Jax asked and I nodded my head. I sat on the bed and began telling him the story of how I met RJ and what he wanted to know. Then I spent an hour answering every question as Mark joined us.

"Candy, I am not going to die and you do not have to choose," Jax stated as Mark put out an APB for Chase. It wasn't until that moment that I realized I should have confessed to them immediately. "RJ is not someone I want you around again."

Mark glared at me with the I-warned-you eyes, and I nodded as the bellhops came to get my bags and the few boxes I had. Then I walked over and, just to show I was moving on, I signed the annulment papers that said we were never married.

"Did you bring it?" Jax asked Mark, and Mark pulled a folder out and handed it to me.

"What is this?" I asked then I looked down to see the tab labeled death.

"You have known me twenty years. If anything happens to me, I want to know that my wishes will be honored like you did for Chase, when we thought he was dead."

"I don't think I can," I replied as my hands shook. I set the folder on the bed, and tried not to look at it.

"You can, and you will, because you love me."

"It's been fun, Jax, but my future is in California, and I need to go. I wish you and Vanessa the best, even if I hope she trips and falls into a wood chipper. You just take care of you. Took me a long time to get you house broken, don't screw it up."

Then Jax pulled me into his arms. I relished the feel of his hardened chest. Even though my faith seemed depleted as the rain fell against the window, I made a wish.

I wish that Jax could be happy and safe. I want him to grow grey hair like his eyes and laugh as children run circles around him. I want him to have the love of his life by his side and never worry about someone having to honor his wishes at a young age.

"Candy," Jax chuckled, and I let go. "Did you just make a wish?"

"How did you know?" I asked.

"You didn't let go of me for nearly five minutes."

I took his hand in mine and tried to get one more boost of electricity that flowed from him to me.

"Maybe I just wasn't ready to let you go," I whispered. I picked up the folder and walked over to give Mark a hug as well. "Tell our girl that I am sorry for overreacting and I will call her when I get settled in."

I looked back into the room, and silently said it all with a nod and a sad smile. This was goodbye, and surprisingly it was nowhere near as agonizing as I thought. Maybe because even though I would be starting over I knew Jax would always carry me in his heart.

I gave them a wave as Mark stood next to him and placed a hand on his shoulder, letting me know he would take care of him. Then I walked away and headed to say goodbye to my dad.

"Dad," I called out as I got to his house. Chelle came running for me again and I wrapped her up in my arms.

"Come in, Candy," my dad called out. I carried Chelle into the living room to see Chase sitting on the couch, but his blond hair had darkened brown roots.

My mind flashed to all the people who I knew with dark brown hair, and none were a match. Maybe I was overreacting. The weather was changing and he may not be outside as much.

"Hello, asshole," I greeted him and my dad looked shocked.

"I apologize for my daughter," my dad continued as I turned and went to place Chelle behind the gate of her playroom.

I peeked around the corner of the living room. Chase smiled largely at something my dad said, and I noticed an indention in his smile. Chase didn't have cheek dimples. Jax did. I walked into the living room.

"Hey Chase, do you remember which park we carved our names in the tree?" I asked, as something was off.

"Sure, wasn't it over off the pier?" Chase responded and then I walked down the hall to the entryway table and pressed my finger to the scanner under the drawer. It popped open and I took out my dad's gun. I walked back into the room and fired the gun into my dad's couch.

"Candy, what the hell are you doing?" My dad screamed.

"Strike one," I spoke calmly.

"Was it Venice Beach?" Chase retorted and this time he didn't even flinch when I shot the coffee table.

"Get Jax on the line. Candice has finally lost her mind," my dad shouted at Michelle and I heard her dialing.

"You are not Chase," I sneered, and he smirked as he stood up and came toward me.

"You knew I wasn't him, but you needed to see him so badly that a little nip and tuck with some bleach and here he is. You wanted to believe he was back so badly that you made yourself believe I was him."

"Who are you?" I demanded to know.

"Who do you want me to be?"

"Dead. I want you to be dead," I growled. as I pulled the trigger. He lunged for me and we fell to the floor, fighting over the gun. As the struggle continued, I kicked him in the balls, but the smart ass was wearing a cup.

"Bad guys don't always win," I shouted as he tried to point the gun under my chin. He was so much stronger than me. I struggled with sweating hands to hold on to my life and the gun.

Silence fell over the house as the gun was placed under my chin. Then I heard a cane on the hardwood and saw RJ walk in.

"Candice, we came to see how you were, and you tried to shoot my new friend here. Tsk Tsk Tsk. What are we going to do about this? I know, let's call Brooklyn in to see if she can cut you a deal for attempted murder. But wait. Brooklyn can't help you now since you decided to do this in Jersey."

"Fuck you," I shouted and RJ merely smiled.

"Tell me, Candice, have you looked into his eyes yet?" RJ smiled his Cheshire cat grin and I looked into Chase's eyes to see familiarity. He wasn't wearing his contacts and his eyes were brown.

Then the Chase-look-alike put the gun to my temple as he wrapped his hand around my throat. Images flashed as I saw Andrew in him. His face had changed, but that was him.

Oh, God! Andrew was alive.

"Have you made a decision yet?" RJ asked as I clawed at his hand, and my dad went to intervene when Andrew pointed the gun at him. I couldn't breathe and my eyes saw black spots.

My dad couldn't stand by and watch me die, so he started for Andrew when RJ got to him. Then Andrew forced me to watch as RJ stabbed my dad in the belly.

"No!" I rasped out as Michelle screamed. Chelle was crying in the playroom. I wanted to close my eyes, and not watch my dad die, but they were not giving me a choice.

"You know how to save him, Candice. Make a choice," RJ sneered. He took my cell phone from my purse and snapped a photo to send out with a text.

"Fuck you! You are nothing more than a gardener with an encyclopedia set. I will never have an answer," I whispered as loud as I could while the familiar burn in my throat had returned.

Memories flashed in my mind of how I had handled this before, but I wasn't as strong as I was back then. I didn't have Jax and while I continued to make dumb decisions, I owned those decisions while I tried to find my way.

Sirens sounded in the distance while I fought to pry Andrew's hand loose. He leaned over and placed his lips on mine and I used what energy I had to bite his lip. He raised his hand to slap me when RJ held his cane out to his hand, and shook his head.

"I will be back for my answer," RJ stated as Andrew wiped the blood from his lip, got up, and placed my dad's gun in his pocket.

"You tasted just like I thought you would. I look forward to our next playtime." Andrew smiled, and they walked toward the door. I scurried over to my dad, gasping in air through my coughing. I applied pressure to the wound as RJ and Andrew left, and my world went hazy.

Chapter 27

I paced the northern portion of the waiting room alone. As people filtered in and out in the back part of the room, my body paced the coffee stand. I owned this little area and snapped at anyone who stepped past a select row of chairs. I would pace a few laps and then stop to stare at the sky where the sun was blazing over the city and there was no rain in sight for me to wish on.

I thought about my life and how I had gotten here. If I had been the woman that Chase needed in his life, he would still be here. Had I seen how Jax felt, he might love me now instead of Vanessa, but I understand him wanting someone who loves him fully and doesn't treat him like a third wheel. Had I been a daughter to my dad and not turned away from him when my mom died, I would have gotten more time with him.

Everything that ever went wrong in my life came from a decision I made. Dad always told me I reacted with emotion, without thinking, and yet I couldn't stop thinking now.

"Mrs. Monroe," the nurse called my name and I halted my steps, sneering my lip, and stared right through her. "Can you share the coffee with the other visitors?" She asked and I merely went back to pacing.

"Yes, she is going to get checked out and then go outside for a few minutes so the families can have some peace. Please come and get us if anything changes."

"And you are?" The nurse asked, and I looked over to see Jax standing there with his hands in his pockets. He almost looked like he was wondering how to respond.

You just say your name, moron.

"I'm her husband," Jax replied.

"Yeah right," I hoarsely rasped out under my breath.

"Mr. & Mrs. Monroe, I will call you if anything comes up, but the surgery can take a few more hours," the nurse tried to comfort us.

"I will stay here and call if anything comes up," Eddie stated from the door. "You should try to get some rest, and let the doctors do their job. We have a few hours before we know anything."

"You mean, if his heart holds up," I directed my words at the nurse as I chewed on my nails. "Because you see, the surgery ends if his heart can't take it and he dies. People go into an eternity of nothingness every day because of hospital negligence, so I need to be right here if he tries to pass on. I need to be here to do CPR and bring him back in case you let him die while you are spending time trying to get people to stop hogging a coffee stand," I declared in a manner that had everyone taken aback by my demeanor. "I'm not leaving," I added my two cents in Jax's direction.

"Jax, take her," Eddie called out and I flipped him off. I was picked up like a bride and I fought to get back to the room. Jax got me to the elevator and I bit down on his shoulder till he dropped me, but even with blood seeping through his shirt, he wouldn't let me go.

He crossed my arms in front of me and enveloped me tightly into his arms, as we entered the elevator.

"Let me go," I pleaded, but there was no empathy from Jax. "He is going to die all alone. I have to be there," I screamed. I kicked at his legs while we rode the six floors down to the entryway and Jax picked me up as tears flowed down my face so fast I couldn't see.

Then Jax took me into a room where there were computer monitors everywhere.

"If I let go, you have to promise not to run," Jax stated and I turned to see there were men sitting watching the videos. On the other side of a glass partition, Brooklyn was sitting with a cup of coffee and her feet up in a chair.

"You're bleeding," Kate called out as she walked in behind us. "I will go get a first aid kit," she added, walking off.

"Mark is outside the door waiting for you to try to run. He loves a challenge, so I hope you ate your Wheaties this morning," Jax whispered in my ear as he let me go.

I was seething mad, as I struggled to stop my tears. I could no longer see that line that pointed out who I was angry at. It seemed that my moral compass said I was furious with myself.

"Candice," Brooklyn said, and I spun to look at her. "I'm sorry if I hurt you. I didn't tell you because I was worried how you would take it. I wanted to protect you a little longer, I guess."

I let out a sigh and pulled her into a hug. I loved her even when I hated her, just as I did Jax.

"I need you to stay away from RJ. That is my battle and don't want to see you get hurt from him," Brooklyn whispered, as I released her.

"He said he wouldn't hurt me. That there was something in my eyes, and I believe him."

Brooklyn stared at me for a while, and then her face fell and something became clear to her. Something in her puzzle piece life just fell into place.

"No, he is honest, even if he is a murdering bastard. If he says he won't hurt you, then he won't. I love you, Candice, and for whatever reason, we were brought together. I just want to keep my friend for a while longer."

"I love you too. You are welcome in my home in California anytime you want, but leave the book drama at home," I stated with the only smile I could rustle up.

I turned to see Jax talking to the guys at the monitors and handed them cash. Then they all shook hands and the men got up and left. Jax walked over to the chairs and sat down. He patted the chair beside him and I defiantly stayed standing. He was having none of my bullshit today as he stood up walked over and picked me up. He sat me in the chair and I rolled my eyes as I crossed my arms and shed more tears. I felt like a waterworks factory.

"Look," Jax demanded, and I turned to see what he was pointing at. It was the surgical room my dad was in. I could see him with the tube down his throat. He looked so weak and feeble. The monitor showed his heart rate was weak, but it was still beating.

"Thank you," I whispered after Jax slid me a cup of Tim Horton's coffee. We had only been there a few hours, but I was exhausted emotionally.

"I want you to let the doctor check you out really quick."

Then a man walked in and began his evaluation of my neck that once again carried a handprint in purples and blues across my throat.

"Your wife should be fine, but watch her for the next twenty-four hours for any signs of severe discomfort or loss of air. It might hurt her to talk in more than a whisper, but that should fade over time."

Then the doctor left the room and I stared at the monitor. RJ had stabbed him just high enough to nick his heart, and break mine doing it.

"You should try to sleep. We are going to be here a while longer," Jax's tone was completely monotone. I wanted to hate him. I wanted to cut his balls off and hang them around my rearview mirror as I ran down his whore, but none of those things were me.

"It is exhausting, Jax," I spoke softly, and he nodded his understanding, only he didn't know what I meant. "I have been forcing myself to hate you, but I don't want to do it anymore."

Jax's attention was completely on me as Kate walked over and closed the door so it was just Jax and I in the little area. I took a drink of my coffee and figured when dealing with life and death, it is best not to leave things unsaid. I only hoped I could tell my dad how much I loved him one more time.

"I loved you. I gave you everything I could of myself. I know it wasn't all of me, and you knew it too. I always kept a piece of me reserved for Chase. I think we hoped we could love each other the way two people should because it made a better love story, but we couldn't as long as I held him in my heart, or you held her in your arms. I will always love you, Jax, but I hate you for giving me a reason to hate you."

I shed a single tear as I looked at the monitor and ran my finger over my dad's face.

"I can never thank you for taking care of him when I left. He is all I have left that I can truly depend on. I know I acted stupid and reckless when I ran off with the Chase look-a-like, but the relationship was already doomed to fail, as we were not being honest with each other. You will always be my storm, Jax, but I will never be your lighthouse."

"Candy, I wish you could-," Jax started, when dad's monitors flat lined. I jumped to my feet and let my coffee cup fall to the floor. The seconds ticked by as the doctors rushed to get his heart started again.

My mom flashed in my eyes, as she fought for one more last breath. One more time to say she loved me. One more minute with the man she loved. All she needed was one more heart beat.

So did my dad.

I ran out of the room and down the hallway. I bypassed the nurse who told me to stop running. As sweat poured off of me, I looked for the stairs, since Mark was now blocking the elevators.

"Where are the stairs?" I finally asked the nurse at the entryway.

"Go down this corridor to the end and then go left. When you hit the dead end, you are there. It is the door to the right."

I took off running. I had to get there, I needed to be there when he said goodbye. I wanted to tell him how loved he was. I needed to tell him what an honor and privilege it was to have been his daughter.

I found the door to the stairs and opened it to see Jax waiting behind the door. I had wasted too much time, and he had beaten me to it. I tried to run past him, but his hands wrapped around my waist and spun me back to the door.

"Candice," Jax called out as he turned me. I slapped at him. I had to get upstairs. I had to be there. I needed to save him or I was going to die alongside him. "Candice, calm down," Jax bellowed and I slapped him across the face. I kicked him in the crotch and he dropped to his knees, but I couldn't get up the stairs, as his one arm held me by my ankle. "Candice, your dad's okay, but you have to stay out of that room."

"Go home to your whore and leave me and my dad alone," I screamed hoarsely.

"Damn it, Candice," Jax gruffly yelled as he tried to get up. "Fuck it," Jax stated under his breath as he grabbed my leg and pulled me to the floor with him. He laid his body on top of mine and stared down into my eyes. Then he whispered the words I never thought I would hear.

"Stop running from me, and run to me, Candice. For once in your life, let me be the one. Let me chase you, let me save you, let me be the one that gets you," Jax spoke softly into my ear. "Why would you want to? I'm a flight risk who will just keep hurting you," I asked, because I knew I would just keep hurting him.

"Because you are worth it."

Chapter 28

As the days flew by, my dad had recovered enough to go home and I was on my way to California. I hated saying goodbye to everyone, but I needed something. I just didn't know what that something was.

I straightened the collar on my red halter dress to make sure it was hiding the remaining bruises on my neck. Mark assured me that Andrew would not get away this time, and as much as I wanted to believe him, I couldn't.

I picked up my purse and fumbled for my phone when I saw that I still had the folded up manila folder inside it. The one labeled 'death.' I saw my phone beneath and went to grab it when an envelope slid out of the folder.

I truly wanted to believe that Jax loved me, but I couldn't help but think his words had merely been there because I had once again been a victim, and he didn't want to lose me that way. I wanted him to want me, and I wanted to want him, but the truth behind the lie of why I ran was still there.

One day he could die, just like Chase.

I turned the letter over and read the cover. To the one who loved her last. I was supposed to give this to whoever got my heart, but the letter would never leave me because Jax had my heart.

To the one who gets her heart:

If you are reading this, then you have successfully won over the girl of our dreams. Whether she chose you while I was alive or dead be confident. It is an award winning act to conquer the wall she has up. She is so strong and indecisive that if she gave this letter to you then you were a better man than me.

I decided to write this letter because I once upon a time knew her best. I want to make sure you understand the gift you are being given, and offer some advice so she doesn't get hurt in the end.

Candice is worth more than gold so treat her as such. She shines like a diamond, do not be the reason that she fades. Her eyes are as blue as sapphires, they need to sparkle not be dulled with redness from tears.

Every morning she takes Tim Hortons and she wants it black. Trying to substitute the coffee for any other brand will get you in the dog house. She loves banana-split waffles from the Cafeteria. Make it a Sunday ritual because she will need a break from writing.

When you move in together install a doorbell as people knocking kind of freaks her out.

If you take her camping bring a comfortable sleeping bag because she will spend the entire trip inside the tent hiding from the crickets. If you stay with her she will curl into your arms and snuggle as the chirps carry on outside. It really makes for wonderful camping trips.

When you both have free time take her to the park by the lighthouse and let her make her wishes on the water. At the time I wrote this she had given up on thinking they work so reassure her that they work because they gave her you.

When she gets upset she has a tendency to get sick or hyperventilate. She has done this since her mother died. When she is devastated she holds her breath until she has to gulp air down because she thinks if she holds still long enough whatever has hurt her will pass her by. When this happens take her in your arms and don't let go.

Don't ever cheat on her. We taught her how to use a gun and when to use it. Do not be a victim on the ten o'clock news, be in the lifestyle section of page six with an engagement announcement instead.

Take her to the cemetery to see her mom weekly. If she doesn't she will jump on a rollercoaster of highs and lows. She can't tell anything is wrong, but you will.

Take her fishing with her dad. It is the one thing he always wanted to teach her, but he hasn't because they are still mending a rift between them.

Don't ever be the man who makes her cry. Be the man who makes her smile.

Give her your everything, because she gives everything she has to give without reservation. Love her as if tomorrow is your last day with her because you will never know what tomorrow holds.

Treat her with the respect she deserves, or walk away now. Never place her up so high on a pedestal that she can't reach because she will die trying to stay there for you.

At the end of each day take her in your arms and tell her she is the world to you. My greatest mistake was when she ran from me I stopped running. Chase her, catch her, hold her, or whatever it takes. I know it gets old, and tiresome, but fear of intimacy set in when Chase cheated on her and you have to show her she is worth the workout you get going after her each time.

But be warned if she ever runs back to me, I will never let her go.

Sincerely,

Jaxson Monroe A.K.A. the mistake

The one who let her slip away.

I got out of the cab and looked at my little ranch style house. This place brought back more memories than I had ever had when looking at the Chase lookalike.

I rolled my suitcase up the step and pushed in the code on the door. I took a deep breath. I didn't think I would adjust here the last time I came here, but I did. In time, this would feel like home again.

I left my bag near the entrance as I walked inside. I passed the tiny yellow kitchen on my left and my white-walled living room on the left. I went down the little hallway and looked into the master bedroom. There on the bed sat a note next to my shadow box.

Ms. Carson, we found this packing up and wanted to make sure you got it back. Thanks for letting us stay here.

Inside was the first rose petal to fall from the first set of roses that Chase had ever bought me. Beside it sat a four leaf clover Jax had given me when we ventured out to find a new place to wish as kids.

I hugged it to my chest as I lay back on the bed and closed my eyes. I wanted to be like Dorothy in the Wizard of Oz and be able to click my heels three times and repeat 'Everything is all right' and it would be.

"Candy." Jax's voice called out and I turned my head to see him in my doorway.

"What are you doing here?"

"I suppose I could ask you the same question. Why are you still running from me?" Jax asked as he stood there, unbuckling his belt.

"What if we are not supposed to be together?" I asked as he unbuttoned his white button down shirt that was rolled up like he was ready to get to work. His muscles made the rolled cuffs tight and showed off his tan. I bit my lip to hide my racing heart and the words that lingered in the air.

"What if we are?" Jax answered when he finally stood naked before me. Confidence poured off him as he walked over and stood before me.

Jax spread my legs and pulled me sharply to the end of the bed. He reached down and moved my thong to the side and pushed the tip of his cock inside me as I gripped my shadow box.

"Do you want to hold onto those memories or do you want to hold onto me?"

It took only three seconds to decide, and I tossed the shadow box beside me. Jax pushed into the hilt when the box left my hand and I gripped his shoulders as he came over me.

"I want you, Jax," I rasped out as my eyes rolled back in my head. Sweat glimmered off me as this carnal act between two people said more than I wanted it to. I had clothes on as a barrier, just like the wall around my heart, while Jax was naked and open to me.

"Then why are you still running?"

Jax leaned down and kissed my neck as I gripped his body and moaned. He roughly grabbed my shoulders and forced me where he wanted me to go. I was at his mercy and didn't want to be anywhere else.

"You deserve better than me," I whispered in a moan as he rubbed that tight bundle of nerves at the apex of my thighs.

"I deserve to have who I want," he growled as he pushed into me harder and my breasts grew heavy. I wanted him to touch them, to put his lips on them, but it seemed he had other plans.

He leaned up and rolled me onto my stomach so quickly that I couldn't say anything. He pulled my hips up off the bed as my legs locked around his back and pushed into me so fast, I was gripping the sheets as my body spiraled with the need to come.

"Why are you running, Candy?" Jax gritted his teeth as I screamed into the sheets. I was so close, but he wasn't pushing me over. I tried to crawl away, but Jax held me tight. I was trying to run from the intimacy and yet I wanted to drown in this feeling forever.

"Because," I shouted, and Jax pushed into me a little harder, rubbing his fingers all around that bundle of nerves without touching it. My heart was pounding and my body was already at the Nasa count down station. All Jax had to do was touch me and I would shoot off like a rocket.

"Because, why?" Jax demanded an answer and I finally figured out if I wanted to get mine, I had to tell him the truth.

"Because if you died, I would too," I shouted. "Because I love you too much. Because I am okay being the other woman in your life. Because I never want to tell you goodbye."

Jax slowed his movements and lowered me back down to the bed. He rolled me back over as tears streamed down my face. I was more wound up than a Timex and it was starting to hurt. Jax bent my knees and leaned over me as he pushed back inside my swollen flesh.

"Don't run from love like that. That is true love. I don't plan on dying, Candy, but if it happens, you will be all right."

Then Jax placed his lips on mine and I just let go of the anger, the fear, the anxiousness, and everything else. I closed my eyes when he leaned up he rubbed that tight bundle of nerves and electricity shot through me until I screamed into the night air.

I sat up on the bed, drenched in sweat, as the shadow box fell into my lap. Out of breath and supercharged, I looked around to see it had all been a dream. I stood up on shaky legs, grabbed my suitcase, and brought it to my room.

I tried to shake the event off, but it was stuck to me like the luster of sweat. I took out my pajamas, then climbed into the shower. I was going to need a cold one to come down off that. Somehow, I believed that was the universe's way of telling me I would never get over Jax.

Chapter 29

A knock on the door woke me from my sleep. I nearly fell off the bed trying to see the clock telling me it was way too early to be up. The knock sounded again and I put on a sweater over my tank and went to the door.

"Good morning, sunshine," Kate stated as I opened the door. Her blond hair shined in the sunlight, which reflected into my squinting eyes.

"You better have coffee," I sneered. Then she handed me a box full of Tim Horton's coffee. There must have been ten or twelve bags. I opened my door a little more to allow her inside. "What are you doing here?" I asked, and she frowned as she saw the inside of my house.

"Seeing how the mighty have fallen, apparently," she responded as she pulled off her coat.

"What are you really doing here?" I asked and she smiled.

"How about you go get a shower and put on some clothes, and I will make your precious coffee so I am not talking to the walking dead. Then we can discuss why I am here."

I groaned as she walked in. I went to take a cold shower to wake me up, and help me remove Jax from my head, as he invaded my dreams night after night. When I was finished, I heard laughter in my living room and went out to inspect, seeing Kate on her phone.

"I'm not waiting for you, so hurry up," she stated as she saw me round the corner. Then she hung up the phone and looked me over from head to toe. "What the hell are you wearing?" she asked and I looked to see I had put on a white ribbed sweater and overalls.

"What?" I asked, and she shook her head. "You are lucky I even match at 6am."

Then she took my hand and led me to the bathroom, where she did a complete makeover. I looked like a Miss America contestant when she was done. Then she forced me out of my overalls and into a black tank top with a white sweater that hung down to my knees, a pair jeans and my Uggs. Just like I used to wear when I lived here before.

"Why do I look like I am headed to a modeling audition?" I asked.

"I need to talk to you, and I wanted to see the beauty you have instead of feeling sorry for you because you look like a hobo. Now let's get down to it. We bought your house."

I nearly got whiplash when she said someone bought my house. I was living in it and never put it up for sale.

What the hell had she laced her Skittles with?

"What the hell are you talking about?" I yelled.

"Awe, Kate did you blow the surprise?" Brooklyn called out as she stuck her head inside the bathroom and then wolf whistled at me. "I can't fit in there, so come out here."

I was seriously concerned as to how much they had had to drink this morning. They were in California, and Brooklyn had two bottles of wine in her hands as we walked to the living room.

We all got into the living room and as soon as I sat down, the phone rang. I got back up and went to the bedroom to grab it, seeing a 212 area code. New York was calling.

"Mrs. Carson," a woman spoke softly over the phone.

"This is she," I answered as I heard the rustling of papers in the background.

"Mrs. Carson, I am Mrs. Kinsey. I am a realtor here in New York County and was calling to congratulate you on the sale of your home."

I peeked around the corner into the living room to see Brooklyn setting out cups.

"What house?" I asked quietly, so Brooklyn and Kate didn't overhear.

"7017 Princeton Lane," Mrs. Kinsey immediately replied. "I just need to get some information so the money can be deposited, as the house was paid off when it was sold. You will receive everything except my commi-"

I hung up on her and walked into the living room, where they were celebrating, and I was fuming.

"You. Bought. Jax's. House!" I enunciated each word precisely as I gritted my teeth.

"Surprise," they shouted and cheered with noise makers. Slowly they calmed down as my face didn't change. I wasn't happy. They bought the house that Jax and I shared for a minute. They now owned my library and the hardwood floor that the moon danced across where the rain puddled inside the window.

I was torn between wanting to cry and wanting to be angry.

"Candy," Brooklyn said softly as I stared through her. "We bought the house for you."

"What?" I asked, because I was sure I heard that wrong.

"Whatever happened between you in the hotel caused him to put the house up for sale. He had paid for the house in full when his parents died, and wanted all the money from the sale to go to you. We didn't want you to lose the house so I went to my mistaken sperm donor, and Brooklyn went to her dad, and surprise." Kate spoke up as she went to hand me the key.

"I have a house here, why would I need it?" I asked.

"You will want it when you get your man back?" Brooklyn explained. I rolled my eyes and let out a sigh. I couldn't be mad at them for trying to do something sweet.

"I am not going to go back for Jax. That ship has sailed. I really appreciate the gesture, but I don't want the money, and I am not going back to New York."

"You don't have to go to New York. They are getting married on the beach in Malibu next weekend. You have seven days to decide what you want or lose him forever. The house is yours either way."

"He doesn't want me anymore," I spoke softly. "I screwed everything up and lost him. I didn't fight for him, or be his partner. I bailed on him over and over again."

"So then knock it off," Kate interrupted my woe is me trip, where I once again took all the blame for what happened between Jax and myself. "That man lights up when you enter a room. His eyes seek you out, not Vanessa. She is a decent enough runner-up, but I think if we took a cheese grater to her face, she would no longer be what he wanted to look at."

"I don't want to talk about this anymore," I whispered.

"Let me tell you what life is like without those you love. I lived it for a year in witness protection. You are trapped in this invisible box where everything and everyone moves in a fast forward pace while you are standing still. It is the loneliest place to be. You will have good days where you think you will survive, and then there are the bad days when you wonder if death would be better than the life you are living. That is what your future holds if you walk away from the one you are meant to be with."

The rest of the day was spent shopping and showing Brooklyn and Kate around Los Angeles, and listening to them complain about how it was not Manhattan. After dinner, I dropped Kate and Brooklyn off at the airport, only to have to return and get them.

"What did you two do?" I asked as we got inside the car.

"I didn't do anything," Brooklyn immediately chimed in, which left all eyes on Kate.

"The security guard groped me so I shoved a Skittle up his nose. I still maintain it was done in self-defense." Kate tried to defend herself, but there was no defense to putting a man that looked like the Rock in a headlock and shoving Skittles into his bodily orifices.

"How long are you here for?" I asked, and Brooklyn sighed.

"I can fly out tomorrow, however Kate cannot fly until they clear her off the no fly list. I have some friends I can call for favors, but it might take a few days," Brooklyn replied and just like that I was stuck in California, in a two bedroom Barbie house, with the two of them.

"Kate, you are sleeping on the couch!" I spoke with annoyance and we drove back to my place.

Chapter 30

I lay on my bed avoiding sleep. Jax coming to me in my dreams over and over again was really starting to take its toll. Sometimes it was hot, but sometimes he was in a coffin, calling out to me. I needed to find closure with everything that happened and move on.

Brooklyn and Kate had been with me nearly a week, and were staying to attend Jax's wedding. Jax was in town, but he never came to see me. I never went to see him. Every time I closed my eyes, Jax was there in memory.

I put on my favorite white halter dress that flared with a bell bottom. I added my lighthouse necklace, and gathered up flowers from the yard and tied them with a piece of lilac ribbon. Then I walked out the front door and got in the cab.

Twenty minutes later, I was at the cemetery when a storm began rolling in. As the sun faded behind the clouds and the sky opened up, I held my arms out in the rain and welcomed it.

I closed my eyes and faced the water, making a wish on the water as my faith refilled.

I wished that I could live happily ever after and Chase would be with us in spirit. I wished I could see him one more time and tell him how much I loved him. I wished that Jax would maintain the peace he found in the death of his best friend.

I felt an arm on mine and turned to look at Jax who was drenched in his suit and tie. His squared jaw and chiseled physique reminded me of why I fell so hard for him, but when his eyes lit up and his cheek dimples showed, I saw the kid in him and those were the memories I relished.

I walked with him over to the red oak tree that hung over Chase's tombstone, and there a minister waited. Brooklyn and Kate were waiting under a tent with Mark and Eddie while Jax and I got married next to Chase's grave so we could have our best man nearby.

I spoke my vows, and kissed my husband as the minister took the papers to turn in, and the rain stopped pouring.

"You have always been the one for me," Jax whispered.

"I will always run to you," I replied, and hugged his arm while the minister talked to him. I turned to see the sun peeking through the clouds and it showed a shape on the ground that made me turn completely around.

Jax turned to see what I was looking at and there, in the overcast, we saw Chase. He was a shadow of color, but we could make out his face as a light surrounded him like an aura.

I smiled the biggest smile I could at him and grabbed Jax's hand.

"Do you see him?" I asked and Jax took a step forward and nodded his head at Chase. Chase then blew me a kiss and nodded his head back at Jax. If I closed my eyes, I could feel him. I felt the warmth Chase always had, and could hear the beats of his heart.

"I see him," Jax called out and soon everyone was behind us.

"Someone call the exorcist or something," Kate stated and I wanted to slap her. I didn't want anyone to move or breathe because he might disappear.

"I promise to take care of her always," Jax said to Chase, and he stepped forward and looked into my eyes with what looked like tears. Then he placed his hands on my belly and a light shined bright.

"I will always love you," I whispered, and another tear fell. Chase evaporated as the storm clouds cast the sun back behind them. "Goodbye," I called out, as I cried out for him.

I sat up off the bed and yearned to hold Jax in my arms from this dream. Bringing Chase in left my heart ripped open. I grabbed my purse to take a sleeping pill so I wouldn't dream anymore. I opened it to see the envelope. The one addressed to me in the event that Jax died. With the ever after fresh on my brain and the need to self-torture, I opened the letter and slid down beside the bed.

Candice,

If you are reading this, then I wasn't able to keep my promise to always be with you. I didn't want to leave you, I never have, but life never asks us what we want.

I want you to know that you held my heart before I even knew your name. You with your sweet toddler voice used to make me do all kinds of things I didn't want to, but I did them without complaint just to see you smile.

Every laugh and cry that we shared as we grew together brought me closer to you. It wasn't until we were both ten and starting middle school that I realized I loved you in a way I shouldn't as your friend.

You may not see it, but you are the strongest woman I have ever known. You set your mind to something and you drive on through to get what it is you want. It was how you stole my heart from me, and wouldn't allow me to share it with any other.

I may have dated women or even told them I loved them, but it was a lie. I couldn't ever give them my heart because you had it all along.

You are the reason I was able to heal when my parents died and when Chase passed away. You thought I was being strong for you, but in reality you pulled me through because you refused to allow it to defeat you. You always thought you were putting too much on me, but in all honesty I needed you to be there every day. I needed to feel the light shine from you. You stayed until that blissful night that I will never regret. Even though it wasn't my name you called, it was my heart you molded to yours and our beats became one.

I don't want to leave you in pain, just as much as I didn't ever want to leave you. I could fill the pages of a book with all the things I want to say to you, and express to you to tell you how much I love you, but the truth is you already know.

I don't have to tell you how I felt, because I showed you every day I could. When my last breath came I hope you were there holding my hand, but if you weren't then my final words to you are that you were always my lighthouse and I will always be your storm.

I will love you through eternity

Jaxson

I paced my house, an emotional wreck, as I held his goodbye letter in my hands. I needed to talk to him, but he was getting married today.

"Fuck it," I said to no one and called a cab. I put on a black bra and my garter with thigh highs. I got dressed into a black rockabilly dress and a pair of black heels.

I grabbed a note pad as the cab pulled up and honked its horn. I tried to write what I needed to say in case they had already begun the ceremony and I wasn't able to tell him anything.

We pulled up outside the Malibu West Beach Club where familiar faces were walking in and out. They had lined the ceiling with lavender flowers that hung on vines. The tables were dressed with white and purple.

I hid in the corner, looking for Jax, as people mingled and socialized. I caught dirty looks and heard the murmurings of 'why is she here?' I felt an ice cold hand touch my back and I jumped when I saw RJ was standing to my right.

"I should pick up a fork and stab you for hurting my dad," I whispered as I pulled his hand off me.

"You should, but you won't."

"Why are you here?" I asked, and he smiled when Brooklyn came into view. I watched him watch her and it all became clear. "You love her, don't you?" I asked.

"Once upon a time I loved her, but you as an author should understand that stuff happens and it is not always a happily ever after."

"I get that part, but if you love her, why do you want her dead?" The silence was eerily seeping into my core as I remembered everything everyone told me about him. "You know, RJ, I think you were once a good person. So tell me, why do you want to hurt anyone?"

"I do not owe you an answer for that."

"You owe me something because you stabbed my dad and were going to let Andrew kill me," I growled.

"I will help end your pain with the information you have been looking for. When Chase died, it was on the steps of the courthouse, in Jax's arms. He didn't make it off the steps to the ambulance. Andrew made contact through a mutual acquaintance. See, he fell in love with you, but you didn't want him, so he wanted you dead. I like to see games played out so I paid for his surgery and allowed the dominos to fall where they were stacked, but I quickly grew bored because while I like to play, all he wanted to do was kill.

"I decided he could no longer work with me and I am getting rid of him."

"What do you mean, you are getting rid of him?" I asked as my heart raced in my chest and my palms grew sweaty.

"I will kill him," RJ replied, as simply as if he was asking for a glass of water. I swallowed hard with his admission.

"I get your role in this was to play some game, but why her? Why me?"

"Brooklyn is my forget me not. You were just a bonus. You see, you kept running from your protector which makes you a target. I have never seen anyone run from their safety net, which intrigued me. Seemed like when Chase died, your internal magnet flipped and you were fighting Jaxson's magnet. After these events though, I think you will find that your role is flipped again and running to him is a lot easier."

I looked over at Brooklyn as Mark joined her and nodded my understanding, even if I didn't understand what exactly the point was behind it all.

"Brooklyn is lucky to have someone like you looking over her," I whispered and RJ seemed to smirk, but quickly dropped it. "I mean, it is really shitty you want to kill her, but it seems you care about her and her friends a lot more than any other killer I have ever read about."

"Don't believe everything you read. I would rather play games than kill, but when the pawns stop playing, it is over. They don't bounce back when they give up."

"Why are you here? Brooklyn and Mark will put a bullet in you if they see you."

"I came to see if your magnet flipped. I want to see if you are willing to go the distance or if you are too broken to play. Mark and Brooklyn only see me when I let them, and today won't be one of those days."

RJ then pulled a corsage that was covered in lilac roses, blue forget me nots, and baby's breath. He placed it on my wrist.

"This has a mic in it. You will need it if you are going to get him back because he is on the beach, as they are getting ready to begin."

"Thank you," I whispered and RJ smirked.

"Don't mistake this for kindness. You are merely a pawn and I need to know if you can still play along."

Then RJ disappeared into the crowd as they all headed out to the beach when the music began playing.

Chapter 31

"Dearly beloved," the minister started as I took off out the front door and ran down the path. I had to push people out of my way until I came to the alter. "Is there any reason why these two should not be married, please speak now or forever hold your peace."

"I have cause," I spoke and the corsage squealed as the microphone turned on. Vanessa was wearing a short white silk dress with lilies in her hand. Her long blond hair flowed down her back. When she looked up at me, she looked happy to see me, which made me stutter.

"You have cause?" The minister asked as I looked over at Jax whose face gave nothing away. His white button shirt was tucked into his dress pants, but the sleeves were rolled up and he wore a lilac tie.

"I do have cause," I spoke up and the minister waved me forward. Brooklyn and Kate smiled and nearly danced out of their seats with excitement.

"I am not sure how to do this, and I was working on leaving a letter-type-poem, so I will just read that, if it is okay." I let out a rush of air as my nerves went into overdrive.

"Read your letter," the minister replied.

"To the one who loves him last,

"If you are reading this, then I want to congratulate you on winning the man with half a heart. Because I refuse to release the other half. I want to send you my empathy because you will always live in my shadow. You see, I love him the most. I loved him first and I will love him last.

"I thought I hated him," I continued, as tears filled my eyes. My voice quaked as I stumbled in my speech. Jax met my eyes and I swallowed hard.

"I really wanted to hate him but I couldn't because in reality I hated who I had become without him. I took for granted what I thought was an impenetrable love.

"So, to Vanessa, who thinks she loves him:

You should already know how he takes his coffee, and his favorite place to fish.

You should know how he loves to fuck and where he makes his wish.

You will become a forgotten memory the second you walk away.

Because in his heart is where I staked my claim and where I plan to stay.

If you believe you truly loved him last,

Then look over your shoulder, my dear, you will see I am his past.

I will be his present for all the days in my life.

His future is filled with days where I will be his wife.

So, I ask you please, if you think you loved him best, to step aside and put it to the test.

He will pick the one who loves him best and put the choice to rest."

"You will merely run again," Jax called out and I smiled at his response.

"I will," I replied, and he turned to look at me.

"Why would I want to keep chasing you?" Jax asked, and I put my hand up.

"You won't have to. I want to spend the rest of my life chasing you."

The crowd gasped and people were talking. I turned to look over at Mark when I started to shake and thought I was going to vomit. He motioned his hand to walk toward him.

"I haven't done much that I am proud of in the last few months, but you and I both know we are not done." Then I turned and looked at Vanessa as I walked slowly. "I am so sorry to do this to you twice, but I need him in my life."

Jax said nothing and tears began to fall from my eyes. I fell to my knees at his feet and begged.

"Please don't make me an 80's romantic movie where I have to stand outside a window with a radio over my head. Please don't make me walk over a Lego pit or shards of glass. Please don't leave me empty without you. I will do whatever you want if you will come back to me and let me make this right, but I am begging you to look inside your heart and if I am still there, then love me back. Take me in your arms and hold me close. Never let me go again. I promise you I will be worth it."

Vanessa's smile fell when Jax looked over at her and there was some kind of silent conversation being had. I stood up and turned to leave as tears fell down my cheeks, when I saw my dad sitting in the chair next to Michelle. Then I looked and saw cousins on my mother's side. I looked over and saw my high school friends sitting in the back.

I glanced at Brooklyn and whispered, "What is this?" She pointed her finger at Jax. I turned around and Vanessa was right behind me.

"This is all for you. Jax set all of this up to get you stop running. You see, he never loved me, not like he loves you. You needed to see what you were losing to find your way home. Be glad you have a wonderful partner who knows you well enough to know that you would come back for him. You are not hurting me, sweetheart. I am engaged," Vanessa spoke sweetly as she waved her finger over at some guy in the crowd.

Then she handed me her bouquet and ran to him. Mark stood up and walked me to the back of the aisle while they reset everything and I couldn't breathe.

What the hell just happened?

"Were Kate and Brooklyn really on the no-fly list?" I asked Mark and he laughed.

"Only for a minute. But we need a minute to reset. I will be right back. I am going to help the minister," Mark stated and I took a deep breath.

"Breathe, Candice, this is what you wanted, and like I said, I love to watch the pawns play games," RJ whispered into my ear.

"How did you do this?" I asked and he smiled.

"Hints were obvious when you re-read your stories. I merely gave it a try, and you missed every clue. This is your do-over with the clues out in the open. Enjoy your new life. I hope to read about it in one of your books one day. Someday, I will want the favor returned, and you will return it because the only reason you have a husband is because I stopped his murder. Never forget that," RJ gruffly whispered.

Jax walked down the aisle to me as RJ took off. He walked up and pulled me to him, placing his lips on mine. I molded to his body as if doing it on command. His hands roamed down my body and came to a halt on my hips. Then he pulled back and I saw the look in his grey eyes that had been there all along.

He took my hand and waved at Mark. They shared something as Jax and I walked inside the venue. Then we walked along the wall to the bathroom and Jax opened the door as I walked inside.

"Get out, we need to talk," Jax demanded all the women leave and then flipped the lock on the door. He turned and looked at me with a predatory smirk as he came near me. My heart fluttered and thrill set my veins on fire. Then, when he was close enough I reached around and spanked him on the ass.

"That is for tricking me into thinking you were marrying some slut-puppy." I rushed the words out, but he only seemed enticed.

"Should I spank you for wearing stockings to my wedding? You knew I wouldn't be able to resist them, didn't you?"

"Spank me?" I asked and he smirked. "You are not the type," I giggled.

"Every man is the type when they want to be," he retorted. "Are you ready for this?"

I nodded as he dropped to his knees in front of me, and spread my legs. He didn't even bother to take off my underwear. He merely moved it to the side like in my dream. I sucked the air in through my teeth when I felt his tongue slide across my clit. I had nothing to grab except him, but his hands grabbed my wrists and held them against the wall.

I was pinned, at his mercy, and loving it. His tongue was heaven as it stroked me in all the right places, just as he knew I needed it. He was mine and I was his. At least, I thought we were.

"Jax, um- are we-oh God-uh- getting married?" I rambled out as my toes tried to curl in my shoes. Then he sucked my clit into his mouth and I screamed as my legs felt weak. "I'm going to-" Lightning shot through my veins and I collapsed to the floor.

"Oh no, I'm not nearly done," Jax stated, as he stood me back up and leaned me over the sink. My body was still tingling from the orgasm that only seemed to break the ice.

Jax ripped my underwear off, and it faltered the hold I had on my body. I watched in awe as he unbuttoned his pants and dropped them behind me.

"Tell me you want me," Jax instructed.

"I do," I cried, with unleashed need. Jax smacked my ass and I groaned as I needed more. "I need you, Jax. I want you so bad it hurts."

Then Jax wrapped my hair into his hand and pushed my dress up with the other. I felt his free hand move around to the front of me and guide him inside me smoothly. It was as if my body obeyed whatever he wanted. Then he pulled out and, as he slammed back in, he pulled my hair back and I cried out.

I closed my eyes and reveled in the way he always changed how we were intimate, and how I was never left unsatisfied. That was something even Chase could not do.

"Watch us," Jax called out as he pulled my hair again, and I watched as his hips moved back and forth. I could nearly taste the orgasmic bliss that was forming inside me. The way he had me was some kind of erotic fantasy where he controlled everything and I didn't have to worry about a thing.

The way we have always done it.

"Fuck," I cried out as I tried to grip anything, but there was nothing to hold onto that would keep me from being sucked under the orgasm that was going to leave me comatose.

"Ahh," Jax groaned when I tightened down on him. If this climax was going to push me over a cliff, he was going down with me. "Fuck, Candy," he called out and I smirked, but it faded the second his finger found my clit once more.

"Jax," I screamed, as it was all coming to a head. The electricity was turning my veins to fire as my breaths grew short and my heart raced to keep up. I couldn't stand up as my legs went numb, but Jax held me in place.

When sweat broke out across his upper lip, I knew he was closing in on it, as was I. I used every ounce of energy I had to push back against him and I heard him grit his teeth.

"Taste me," I called out and Jax looked in the mirror at me.

"I have created a dirty-vanilla girl," Jax smirked. Then he pulled out of me and I wanted to scream and pound my fists, but instead he grabbed the edge of his pants, and carried me into the carpeted dressing area, where he got down on the floor.

My legs were so weak that I couldn't do much and Jax seemed to know because he laid me down and climbed over me. He immediately licked the apex in between my legs as I took his cock to the back of my throat and swallowed.

I could taste myself on him and the thought crossed my mind that it would always be me on him. Then I felt a finger go inside me and brush that rough patch that carries all the secrets of women. I felt a second finger graze it and screamed around his length. I reached up and cupped his balls and he began pumping into my mouth in rapid succession. He swelled in my mouth and I could taste the pre-cum all over. I knew he was going to go any second and I was trying like hell not to, but then it was too late.

The orgasm burst through me and left me moaning and squirming all around his hardened cock in my mouth. I reached my hands up and grabbed his butt and brought it down and as deep as I could. The more the waves hit, the harder I sucked to keep from screaming.

Then the first spirt hit and I swallowed it down quickly. He kept pumping into me until I was licking him clean. Then he rolled off me and lay beside me, holding my hand.

"Do you want to marry me?" Jax asked as we struggled to catch our breath. "I mean, I know I put this all together, but if you don't want to..." his voice trailed off.

"I want to be your wife more than I want water to hydrate, or oxygen to breathe. I don't even have to marry you, Jax, as long as you are mine and I am yours."

Chapter 32

Jax and I had tied the knot, broken the glass, and lit the candle. The minister took the paperwork and turned it in so there would be no repeat of last time. The reception was wonderful so far, with everyone congratulating us and telling me their role in bringing us together.

"I am running to the ladies' room," I softly told Jax.

"Hurry back or I will chase you in there," Jax whispered in my ear as he winked. He let me go so he could talk to Vanessa and her fiancé, who both seemed very happy with each other.

A few moments later, I heard the toilet flush and water run. I walked out of my stall and was washing my hands when I felt someone behind me.

"Hello, Candy," Andrew called out and I looked up in the mirror to see he still looked somewhat like Chase. "Smells like you gave someone what is mine in here."

"There is nothing in here that is yours," I growled, as he smirked. He then grabbed me and, without much strain, he threw me into the mirror. The blow to my head left me hazy to what was happening.

Andrew then pulled me off the sink by my hair and let me drop to the floor. He picked me up, spun me around, and forced me on my knees.

"Beg," he challenged, and I tried to get up, but he backhanded me. "I said, beg for your life," he bellowed.

"Fuck you," I replied and he slammed my head back against the wall. I tried to get up, but I couldn't. Everything was going in and out of focus. I pulled my hands up to shield my face and talked into my flowers. "Help me," I softly whispered, hoping the mic was on. "He's going to kill me."

"Who are you talking to, bitch?" Andrew hit me again and my body flew to the floor. When I got back up, I tried to punch him in the dick, only for him to grab my hair and drag me across the floor. I looked over to see a blood trail from me on the white tile.

He pulled me into the dressing room and propped me up on the bench. The room was spinning and I was exhausted, as darkness was trying to consume me. I pulled my wrist away as Andrew unzipped his pants and I spoke again.

"He's going to kill me now. Tell Jax I love him." Then I dropped my arm as Andrew forced me back onto my knees by my hair.

"I should have killed Jaxson and you when I killed Chase. But I have plans for your mouth."

It wasn't seconds later that I saw three of Jax in my vision. He threw Andrew across the room and Andrew charged him when he got back up. Brooklyn was beside me in an instant.

"Are you okay?" She asked, as I watched Jax punch Andrew in the face.

"Where is RJ?" I asked, and Brooklyn looked at me with a deer in the headlights look. "He promised he would take care of him. He lied."

"Get an ambulance," Brooklyn called out and Eddie was in my sight in a moment's notice. The

NYPD guests rushed in and helped Jax restrain Andrew while the LAPD came to pick him up.

"She has lost too much blood," Eddie called out as he tied off my thigh. I saw a piece of the mirror sticking out of my leg and wondered how it got there.

My head felt heavy and the pain was excruciating. I wanted everyone to stop talking and turn out the lights, but I couldn't talk myself. They placed me on a stretcher and put me in an ambulance with sirens too loud.

Eddie threw out the medic from the back and went to work on me. Jax climbed in the back and held my hand as they tried to get an IV started.

"Get her dad and meet us at the hospital," Jax shouted. Then a shot rang out and Jax covered me with his body. I could hear the screams and the stampede of people running. Everyone was looking for a sniper on high as RJ walked right past the ambulance doors and smiled at me.

Brooklyn shut the ambulance doors and Jax shouted for the driver to get me to the hospital. Then everything went dark.

Everything was still dark, but I could hear thunder in the distance. Then I heard Jax talking.

"I'm not sure how this works, but Candy always wishes on the water and somehow the storms feel what she feels. They seem to be in sync with her."

"Make a wish for my daughter to wake up. It has been three days and they said that it is up to her now. I can't lose her," my dad said, and I fluttered my eyes, only to get blasted with bright lights and a headache from hell.

"I don't want to screw it up. Do you know how she started?" Jax asked.

"When my mom used to tell me about them, I merely made a wish and drenched myself in the water," Brooklyn spoke up, and I was in awe that they were trying to make a wish on the water for me. I heard glass shatter and then Brooklyn spoke.

"Please don't take Candy from us. She is part of my family. If I never make another wish, let me have this one. Please don't take her from us."

I heard crying as I attempted to open my eyes again. I tried to talk, but my throat was not allowing it. I fluttered my eyes open again, and this time I got them parted enough to make out fuzzy people.

"I wish you could find a way to save my wife. Please don't take her from me when I just got her. Please don't take our baby. Let her wake up or take me instead. Let her live on and if you need a soul to fill your quota, take me. I have loved her my whole life and want her to live knowing how cherished she really is. Please let her wake up," Jax begged.

They were all staring at the window and it was then I noticed the rain was ponding on the white floor. I saw my dad in a chair, weeping. Jax and Brooklyn were standing in the water by the window. Eddie was looking over my chart, and Kate was crying as leather man comforted her.

I whimpered when I saw him and I heard a gasp. Then Jax was in my line of sight as everyone surrounded me. I kept looking over at leather man, and then back to Jax.

"Call Mark on his cell," my dad called out. "Wasn't he going to talk to the doctor?"

Brooklyn picked up her phone and everyone hovered around me.

"Hey honey, are you with the doctor?" I heard Brooklyn ask. "Tell him she's awake and to get his ass up here, New York style."

I squeezed Jax's hand and looked over at leather man again, and thankfully Jax caught on.

"That is Maverick, he is Eddie's brother. He works for the DEA. He was undercover working for Andrew while he gathered evidence."

Then I looked over at leather man and he showed me his badge. Kate put her hand on his shoulder as if she knew him, but she had said nothing at the restaurant. I frowned at her.

"I am really sorry about shooting your husband. I had a role to play and if I hadn't, we would all be in coffins by now. I hope you understand my intent was never to hit him, but to merely scare him."

Jax gave me a smile that said all was forgiven on his end, but it wasn't on mine. He shot my husband. Job or no job, there are lines you do not cross. Before another word could be spoken, the doctor walked in.

"Did you really break the window?" The doctor asked and Jax nodded.

"Yes sir, and I will pay for it," Jax responded.

"Let's start with the patient. How are you feeling?" He asked, but my throat was so dry and gruff, I felt like if I tried to speak, I would be ripping my flesh. He called for something and the nurse brought it in. He sprayed the back of my throat and then had me drink water behind it.

"Better?" he asked.

"Yes," I said as it came out in a softened whisper. Then he made me follow his light and did other routine tests to see where I was.

"I want another CT, and OB will need to come check her again. We will keep you another day or two to make sure you are okay, but this crew you brought from New York should stay on their side of the Mississippi after this visit."

I nodded my head and they all rushed me to hug me. When they were finished, my dad sat on one side and took my hand in his.

"No more killers outside of books. My heart can't take it, and with my grandchild on the way, I want you wrapped in bubble wrap."

"Grandchild?" I asked and then my dad smiled as he looked over at Jax.

"It seems that your pill couldn't withstand the army I sent in. You are a couple months along. We got pregnant on the honeymoon, it would seem."

I pulled my arm over and placed it on my belly. I was going to have a baby with Jax, and was overcome with emotion because I finally had everything I ever wanted. I had my family and friends. I had Jax and now I would have a baby. Most importantly, I no longer felt a need to run from any of them, and my faith was restored when I heard them wishing on the water for me.

Chapter 33

"You know RJ shot and killed Andrew." I spoke softly to Brooklyn as everyone went to clear out the California house so we could sell it.

"I know, but that does not vindicate him from all the wrong he has done. When I catch him, he will die or he will be found guilty in a court of law."

I ate the Jell-O they had brought me. One more day and I would have been in this hospital a whole week, and I was going stir crazy.

"Do you think you could be an escape queen for me right now?" I asked, changing the subject and Brooklyn latched onto it immediately.

"What is it you need?" She asked. "You are not trying to get me to bring Kate in here so you can steal her Skittles again, and then yell at her for not telling you who Maverick was, are you?"

"Stealing her Skittles is going to happen again and again, but right now, I want a Snickers. I already talked to her about the other. She didn't know who he was until the shooting. Eddie didn't even recognize him, they said."

"All right, honey, tell me what you want." Brooklyn smiled at me.

"I want to go home. I don't want to be here another day. But Jax will say no if I try to sign out AMA."

Brooklyn seemed to be thinking it over as we sat silent for a moment. Then she got up and walked out of the room. When she came back, my Jell-O was gone, and she had a wheelchair.

"I am not stepping into that between you and Jax, but it is raining. How about a trip to the roof?"

I nodded and Brooklyn took me upstairs. When we got to the roof, I tilted my head back and let the rain pour down on me. I had never felt so alive.

"Brook?" I called out and she walked around to stand in front of me. "You were there that day. Did Chase die on the steps of the courthouse?"

She opened her umbrella and knelt down in front of me.

"Candy, I was rushed to safety, so I wasn't there, but from the video I saw, I could say yes. Jax started CPR, but blood started to blow out of Chase's chest because it had pierced his lung. Then you see Jax take Chase in his arms. Chase moves his lips, and you can see Jax fighting back tears. They almost had to pry him away from Jax because he was already gone, and Jax wasn't ready to let go."

Then Brooklyn took my hand and I could see the red rimming her eyes as a tear fell down my cheek.

"It is cruel what Andrew and RJ did by letting you think that Chase was alive and hiding from you, but I had the judge sign the order to exhume the body, and I stayed with them while they did it. Chase was inside the casket. I am so sorry, honey."

Then Brooklyn pulled me into her arms, and I burst into tears. Even though it was cruel, I wanted it to be real because I wanted my friend and confidant back. I wanted him to know his daughter and grow old with us.

"How did Andrew-?" I cut off as more tears fell from my eyes and I was gasping for breaths.

"He broke into your house and took the photo, diaries, and everything else he could get his hands on to know your history together. They found it all when they raided his home. The blood at the scene was Chase's from when they prepped his body for burial. The mortician and his staff have been charged for it."

I put my hand over my mouth and cried. The rain seemed to pour down harder the more I cried. Brooklyn enveloped me into her arms and I shattered. Healing from a lifetime bond was going to take more than a year, it seemed.

The sun pierced through the sky and shined down on me as the rain stopped. I could feel Chase's warmth in the rays of light. I thought back to my dream and wondered if it was a dream, or if Chase was letting me go.

"Brooklyn, take me home," I stated and she nodded her head.

"You sure you want to go out there?" Jax asked. We had been back in New York for about five hours and it was time to go to the cemetery. They had put Chase back and I wanted to set flowers there.

"I'm sure. I need to do this," I responded. Jax swept me off my feet and carried me out to his waiting truck. Then he grabbed everything I requested from the house.

We rode out to the cemetery in silence. Jax held my hand and I wondered if this was where my life was supposed to have led. When I started to do the what ifs, that was usually what had me running, so I scooted over to sit right beside Jax and took a deep breath to let it go.

When we reached the cemetery, I got out and Jax and I helped smooth the new dirt. Then I took a packet of seeds and poured them all over the top of Chase's burial plot.

"Jax and I are going to name our first son after you, just like you asked. We are going to adopt your daughter and tell her about you every day that she is with us. When you died, I lost my way. I lost it again when I thought you had come back. I wanted him to be you so badly that I forced myself to believe it was you when my heart knew better. I've been holding onto you every minute I have been with Jax, but through this adventure I finally learned how to let you rest in peace. I hope you can see that I am happy and sated now. Good luck on the other side." I said my goodbyes as I would every day for three more years.

Every day for three years, I went to the cemetery, and finally when I took my two-year-old son, Chase, out there today to plant flowers, I saw them.

That one little packet of forget me nots that RJ had left in my mailbox covered half of the cemetery. They would mow over them, but for now, I was going to place fresh flowers on every grave that was calling out to remember them.

It took me longer than normal, as I was pregnant with our daughter and could barely see my feet, but whatever I didn't do today, I would do after I got my word count in during Chase's nap. The books were rolling out of me now that I finally had something to say.

"Time to go home, Chase," I yelled out across the baby blue sky. "Chelle will be off the bus in half an hour."

Chase and I loaded up and headed home where we made it just in time to pick up Chelle, who Jax and I had adopted to raise as our own. No one knew her dad better than we did, and I wanted her to have the best chance at knowing who he was.

"Hey honey, I'm home," Jax called out as he entered the house, two hours later.

"We are learning how to cook from YouTube," I replied, as he started opening windows to get rid of the burnt smell.

"Whatever it is, don't eat it," he chided, as he came in and kissed me on the lips. "Hello, my beautiful wife," Jax stated as he pulled me into a dance.

"Hello, my gorgeous husband." Then my stomach kicked. Jax stopped dancing and dropped to his knees, feeling his daughter dancing away in there. He placed a kiss on my belly when Chase came running up.

"I wanna kiss my baby," Chase called out and I laughed.

"She is going to be here before you know it," I laughed. "Now, both my boys, go get Chelle and get washed up before I order real food and have it delivered."

Jax called for Chelle as he took Chase by the hand and led him into the toddler friendly bathroom. I picked up the mail and opened a letter from my agent that said my book about RJ had made a bestseller list, but it was no surprise. The case files Brooklyn let me see to research him made him seem like a super hero gone bad. I often wondered whatever happened to him, but today I wouldn't.

I opened up a letter with no return address. I pulled it out and a forget me not fell out.

Dear Candice,

I wanted to say I enjoyed your book about me immensely. Perhaps it is time to enroll you in a better adventure and see how it turns out.

Love the flowers,

RJ

"Maybe in another book," I whispered. Then I heard the sounds of laughing children running down the stairs and I dropped the card in the trash and went to play along.

The End...

Or is it?

No, it's the end!

Maybe...

Author *Elizabeth* York

Follow the Author:

FB Page: http://goo.gl/JUeolZ

Twitter: @AuthorEYork

Amazon Page: http://goo.gl/4grbpK

Street Team: https://goo.gl/5g9gcG

Fan Group: https://goo.gl/CMB9cb

Play list:

Available for each book from the Author.